MERIT BADGES

A NOVEL

KEVIN FENTON

New Issues Poetry & Prose

Western Michigan University
Kalamazoo, Michigan 49008

First Edition, 2011.

ISBN-10: (cloth) 1-930974-95-7
ISBN-13: (cloth) 978-1-930974-95-1

Library of Congress Cataloging-in-Publication Data:
Fenton, Kevin
Merit Badges: A Novel/Kevin Fenton
Library of Congress Control Number: 2001012345

Cover Design: Gina Dubay
Production Manager: Paul Sizer
The Design Center, Gwen Frostic School of Art
College of Fine Arts
Western Michigan University

This book is the winner of the Association of Writers & Writing Programs (AWP)
Award for the Novel. AWP is a national, nonprofit organization dedicated to
serving American letters, writers, and programs of writing.
Go to www.awpwriter.org for more information.

MERIT BADGES

A NOVEL

KEVIN FENTON

NEW ISSUES

 WESTERN MICHIGAN UNIVERSITY

To my parents, Agnes Fenton and the late Maurice Fenton. I would not have written this book without them.

To Ellen. I would not have written this book nearly as well without her.

Our friends—how distant, how mute, how seldom visited and little known.

—Virginia Woolf, *The Waves*

. . . this turbulence in breast and breath that indicates a purity residing somewhere in us . . .

—C. K. Williams, "Nostalgia"

PROLOGUE:

The Greatest Moment in Junior High History

Chimes Sanborn: Here is the truth about life in junior high, at least if you're a guy in Minnisapa, Minnesota in the 1970s: you're a monkey and your life is a misdemeanor. You spend eighty percent of your time elbowing your friends or knocking their books on the ground or butting them with your shoulder or pretending to crack eggs on their heads.

This is maybe seventh grade. Some kid from the Catholic school had showed up in his Boy Scout uniform for some bike safety talk, and we had decided that Scouts was for dorks, and we vowed to throw out our uniforms. Of course, we never actually threw the suckers away. Five years later, we'd be playing poker in somebody's basement and see a merit badge sash in a closet, behind the Spirograph.

Sex and booze are rumors; copping a feel in a basement rec room, sneaking some Ripple wine—these are mythic experiences.

We'd all just seen that rerun of the *Dick Van Dyke Show* where his brother shows up and they call each other "Berf." So we started calling each other that.

We're at the Regal Theater, back in the days before the multiplex. A bunch of guys are there. The usual suspects: me, Slow,

Quint King, Burpee. Probably Pooch Labrador.

We whip Dots at the screen because Dots were *designed* to be thrown at movie screens. We also launch the occasional Dot at Barb Carimona and her friends, who are sitting a couple of rows in front of us. They turn and yell but they like the attention. And then, Smash Sarnia, who was born to be in j-high, ups and whips an apple core through the screen. It splats and shatters. It's tremendously cool.

His aunt, who he called Mom because he was an orphan, must have given him the apple. She was always doing that, giving him things from home, so he wouldn't have to buy stuff at the theater, and he was surprisingly cool about it. At this point, life hasn't slapped any of the rest of us yet. This is before Quint King went off the deep end or Slow went off the shallow end. This is before Barb left and came back and left again. This is before just about everything.

We're all just a bunch of monkeys. We played Monopoly to expand our worldview.

It turns out that the apple core itself is only a warm-up for Smash's ultimate act of defiance. A couple of ushers start hauling him out the side exit, and just as they've got him almost out, with his arms pinned behind his back and his feet dragging, Smash—this skinny thirteen-year-old kid—announces "I'VE BEEN THROWN OUT OF BETTER PLACES THAN THIS!" and the entire audience loses it, and it's the most glorious junior-high moment in history, and our entire row of guys starts to howl and cheer, and we all get thrown out, too.

WOODWORK

Make something useful out of wood.

Quint: I was in my jock-strap, ass to the air, stuffing one of those junior high phys-ed shirts—two t-shirts welded together, always mildewy—into a locker, when Mr. Schmertz tapped my shoulder and asked me to get dressed and come outside with him. I'm not sure I showered; as I walked the hallway, the orange lockers grinned and gauntleted me; I stepped outside; the big stone steps descended below me; it had rained, the air was wet and cold, and the sun had come back without improving anyone's mood. I knew that my dad had died as soon as I saw my sister's face.

My sister hugged me and I looked away, over her shoulder. The snow had melted, and the grass was dirty. My sister, in town on break from law school, let me go, and I noticed a mushed pink jawbreaker box, with a plastic window in the center. The air flowed like syrup.

When we got home, ladies were already calling to ask, "Is there anything I can do?" and every time the question felt painful, like a light flipped on, and then food appeared: seven-layer bars, baked ham, scalloped potatoes, crocks of beans, pots of soup, sugar cookies, apple bars, apple crisp, caramel rolls, coffee cakes, roast-beef sandwiches, party platters on that rhubarb-colored glass, ham sandwiches, cheese plates, jars of preserves. It was as if they tried to bring back Dad by showing up with everything he ever ate. I wolfed down an entire plate full of seven-layer bars and my blood dervished and women touched my arm and called me dear and men touched my shoulders and called me son.

The funeral home had plants that had never been outside and wood paneling that reminded me of mannequins. My brother and sister knelt and prayed before the coffin. They cried like they were supposed to: they cried like their souls were rivers. But I leaned over my dad's face and touched his mustache: the little hairs gave a mousy bounce but his paraffin face didn't move. I ran back to where my sister was sitting with her best friend. "Dad wants a cigar," I said. They laughed. I'd made them nervous.

The Polaroid camera was behind my mom's chair. It was the one that Dad, who was a lawyer, was using to take pictures for some lawsuit when he fell off a barge and drowned. When Dad slipped into the water, the camera fell onto the deck. At the funeral parlor, I grabbed the camera and snapped a picture of Dad. It showed him with his hands folded over his white shirt and tan suit, and it made me feel as if we had found his clothes, and his body was just one more piece of clothing. When the Polaroid first slid out of the camera, the developing gunk looked like river mud and then the mud became my dad. A lady I didn't know leaned over my shoulder and said, "He looks peaceful." Her perfume stung my eyes, and I could feel the shadow of her against me and then I could see her embalmed grownup face and I wanted to run out into the air.

At the funeral, I couldn't see anything because I was in the front row and looking straight ahead at the coffin and the lectern. But it felt like everyone was as rigid as soldiers and every once in a while someone would break down and sniffle or sob; but then they would stop and everyone would be rigid again. Everyone envied statues; everyone hated what squirmed inside them.

When we were walking out of the church, I looked down from the grownup faces. My feet moved; the grey carpet flowed. I could feel my sister squeeze me. When I thought we were past everyone, I looked up. I saw my friends in the back row, in their Boy Scout uniforms. They wore their kerchiefs and their badges of rank and their merit badge sashes. Down the row, I caught glimpses: brainy-bland Pooch, goofy-birdy Burpee, crazy-confident Smash were all serious now.

And then I saw my two best friends: Chimes normally reminded me of Bugs Bunny: a skinny kid who simmered wise-cracks. He was stiff with respect. He turned to me and nodded, then looked down. And then Slow looked at me. He held himself like a dad. He caught my eye and raised his hand in a slow salute, which he held as my sister tugged me past.

I started to bawl like a baby.

My brother and sister drove away, and we packed up the last of the food to send with them. I remember wishing there had never been a funeral. The house wouldn't be so quiet and empty.

The world was in a bad mood that summer: The sky was sad, but that's because it's the sky and we like the sky because it's the only thing in the world that's as moody as we are; but trees are something else. The trees were pissed off. You could see it in their scaly and scabbed skin.

And my mom changed. I could tell it when I would come home from playing in this double-elimination Monopoly tournament that Pooch Labrador had concocted. I'd be feeling more than a little weird already because, whatever had happened at the funeral, Chimes and Slow just didn't get how strange the world had become, and Chimes was just a skinny blonde kid and Slow was so clean cut you thought of him in black and white. I don't know where he got off posing as the All-American Boy when we all knew his parents were breaking up.

Chimes and Slow thought they were the cleverest little creatures ever to walk the earth, and I would want to tell them to SHUT UP. The world was too quiet, but whenever they started going on about an alternative universe where everything was the same except for one Monopoly token, I could barely restrain myself.

And when I came home, Mom would be in the living room, with the shades drawn, saying the rosary, and I didn't want to talk to her because she was in some trance, praying, and she would say, "Please lift this burden." I tried to walk like I was an altar boy, like it was my job to carry the cruets of wine and water, to carry the trembling candles, but I never felt quiet enough to make her happy.

One Sunday afternoon, Mom suggested that we go for dinner to the big steak place with the two-story portable cow in the parking lot. Mom and I didn't say anything on the way to Steak Out, because I think we both knew that we didn't have that much to say and we wanted to save it for when we were in public. I was slouched down on my side of the car. I didn't like being with my mom in public, but I couldn't make a big deal of it because it was just her. The kids with Moms and Dads could slink around and tell them, "Don't look like you're with me," and their parents would just chuckle to each other and say, "Remember when we were like that?" But my mom couldn't do that.

I ordered the steak, and the baked potato with what amounted to a lava flow of butter and sour cream, and the salad with the croutons and carrot shavings and vomity blue cheese dressing, and as much runny ice milk as I could fit onto the top of a cone. We tried conversation, like it was a sport we were trying to learn.

"How's your meal, Quint?"

"Good."

Then a little later, I said, "And yours?"

"Very good. Excellent," as if she were being interviewed for a commercial. "I don't know how they prepare these steaks so expertly. And the salad is very fresh, too."

After some more silence, she asked, "How are your friends?"

"Fine. I don't know, they seem a little stupid."

"They've never struck me as stupid. I always thought you were lucky to have such friends."

I couldn't really explain what I meant, so I didn't say anything. The rest of the meal Mom just smiled a lot at me.

Before he died, my dad and I had started building a boathouse. When Dad died, we'd already attached the pontoons to the bottom and built the frame for the walls and ceiling.

There was a clear line between where Dad and I had built it together and where I built it by myself. Dad and I had been a lot neater. The roof was corrugated tin. I nearly killed myself trying to put that on—in the sun, it winked some falcony secret to me—but I did it. Then I built a bunk/couch thing in one corner. I brought a Coleman lantern and some matches from the garage, and put some of my dad's books in there.

I came home one night after the Monopoly tournament, and when I opened the door, she yelled, "DON'T MOVE." There must have been forty Hummel villagers gathered in the living room.

"Just don't move. Don't move. I'll move these."

She gathered up a shepherd girl and a boy blacksmith and a milkmaid and placed them in the center of the room. It took her forever because she carefully rearranged other figurines to make room for them.

"I'm sorry, Mom."

"It's nothing. You just picked a really bad time to come in."

"I said I'm sorry."

"Just walk carefully. It will be fine."

I tip-toed through the living room. I wanted to do a Godzilla on those stupid things.

There were some planks in the front of my boathouse so it had a porch. I sometimes would spend entire afternoons on those planks, on a folding chair that my brother, in a rare moment of non-perfection, stole from a church basement. I would look out on the river. Near my feet, the last things my dad tasted, little green algae things, floated. The river was dirty. Shiny-backed turtles sometimes swam out to a jut of island and stared back at me. In the background, Minnisapa was a mist of trees, and the hills beyond the town were flat and dark. The sky above the hills belonged to some other place.

I spent whole afternoons staring at the river, noticing the way it slapped and shrugged. It was never false; it always had something to say; it always made my thoughts bigger and sweeter, even when they were sad. If you think about it, you know that rivers are graveyards.

One night, we were sitting in Pooch Labrador's basement playing Monopoly among the *National Geographics*, and Chimes said, "We should make a Minnisapa Monopoly board."

"That'd be cool," Pooch and Slow said at the same time.

"Our neighborhood would be like the nice but not stuck-up ones," Slow said. Our neighborhood was a square of two-story houses in the middle of town. It ran from Bunke to Schuth to Marcotte to Munson. When somebody said, "our neighborhood," this is what we all thought of because, when we were little kids, we couldn't cross those four streets without permission. In our neighborhood, there was always a parent of one of us guys within a block—or, if not our parents, somebody like Mr. or Mrs. Carimona or Hubie at Hubie's Foods or one of the crazy old maiden aunts who prayed for us. And when we kept going past the Go Mart on Bunke and Schuth one day, north and east toward the river and then out of town on the weedy old highway, we knew we were doing something we weren't supposed to. We felt naked. We rode our bikes like crazy bugs. All bets were off, and we killed frogs.

"Yeah, the rich dopes across new Highway 61 are Broadway and Park Place," Chimes said.

"And the people on, like, Baltic are dubes like Tulep who live in shacks on the edge of town. And the people on St. Charles are like poor people in the south end, who at least bother to go to church and mow their lawn."

"My dad said that Tulep's old man has a lawn mower on blocks in his front yard," Chimes said. "Couldn't afford a car."

I couldn't stand these guys thinking they knew everything

anymore, so I left, and I just couldn't bear the thought of what delicate scene I might ruin when I came home, so I started to walk down Marcotte Street toward the river. It must have been about ten at night. When I crossed the bridge, the river was about 100 feet below me. The bridge was a carnival ride that broke down and left you hanging in mid-air. All that air curled up and jumped into my gut. I could see the tops of the trees on the islands. The river was brown and moved; the islands were gray and still.

I stayed there a long time, leaning against the rail, watching the river change. Then I walked the rest of the way, crossed the sandy ground and then the plank that connected my boathouse to the land, holding my arms out like wings so I wouldn't fall in. I opened the door and stepped inside.

The darkness swarmed over me like water.

I tripped; I bumped the crazy bone in my knee; I felt for the matches but pushed them off where I couldn't see them. The darkness kept swarming and smothering around me, like water all clotted with weeds and scary with creatures; I thought my heart was going to stop; it felt like I'd been running for ten miles; I crawled under the bed and banged my head; I groped and groped, grasping for anything solid; I smacked my knuckles against wall and it hurt so much I wanted to cry, but I couldn't stop, and then, finally, I grabbed ahold of the matches: I tried to get up calmly and, with my hands shaking, I finally struck a match. The little pouch things in the lantern glowed and made the inside of the boathouse almost safe. I sat and caught my breath and waited for my heart to slow down.

But I still wasn't used to the quiet. The world chirped and splashed and moved. I heard a sound and wondered what kind of animal made it. But I forced myself to stay there. I tried to read, but couldn't; my mind water-skied over the words.

What I'm told was two hours later, my mom showed up with the police. Her face was crazy; she grabbed me. I could smell her perfume and her talc and feel the cross she wore around her neck biting into me, and I could feel her dry soft skin and I could hear her sob behind my head because she squeezed me so hard her head was behind me and she was gasping, "Never do this to me again. Never do this to me again." And then she started making crazy sounds and holding me tighter and tighter and I twisted away from her, to get some air.

COOKING

Slow Slocum: My dad's been a total dube lately. He's been gone even more than usual, and, when he's here, he and Mom have these fights in the bedroom with their TV on so we supposedly can't hear them. That's when I get the rest of the kids, and we play badminton on the side of the house away from my parents' bedroom. And my mom's been even sadder than usual. Right now, she's in her room. It's 5:20 in the afternoon, I'm back from cross-country practice, and I don't think Mom's coming out to make us dinner. I'm afraid to knock. I'm afraid to start making dinner because it would look like I don't trust her.

But *Leave It to Beaver* is going to be over in eight minutes, and my little brothers and sisters are going to be even more stupid than usual. They like *Leave It to Beaver* because they feel superior to it. Not me. I am trying to think what Ward Cleaver would do in this situation but not coming up with much.

There seem to be some kind of sounds coming out of the bedroom. I think Mom is crying. Or maybe not, maybe it's just the normal sounds the world makes. Maybe it's silence, but that's not good either. She's been in there all afternoon. She hasn't dressed yet. It's now 5:26. Brother Number 2, who is the dube to end all dubes, gets bored with *Leave It to Beaver* and starts to strut toward the bedroom door and says, "It's time for Mom to make dinner. Time's a-wasting." I grab him and say, "No." And he says, "Fuck you" and squirms away. And I say, "That's not appropriate language." And he says, "Who appointed you king?" and knocks on the door, and when Mom appears, she looks like someone else, like she's been sleeping for five months; she looks like crying would be too much exercise, and smart little brother doesn't know what to say, and I say "Mom, it's okay. You're tired. I'll make dinner." And she nods and goes back into the bedroom.

I find a box of Hamburger Helper with the creepy smiling hand and figure out the directions and make it, and everybody starts to sit around the table, to the extent that my simian brothers and sisters ever sit anywhere. Then as I'm serving everybody their Hamburger Helper, Brother Number 2 just starts sobbing, and Brother Number 3, who's had two years less practice at being a dube says, "What's his problem?" and I tell him to shut up, and I tell Brother Number 2 that it's gonna be okay, Mom's just really tired, and then I ask everyone to make a list of their ten favorite hot dishes and, when they say things like Rat Eyeball Stew, I just go along with it and let them have their fun, because I noticed that sometimes Ward Cleaver would just chuckle when the boys did something stupid.

And then Brother Number 3 says, "Is that going in with your other lists?" They'd looked in my dresser once and found all my lists, like my "People Who Would Make Star Trek Crew Members" list. I'd revised that one just recently. Quint King had seemed like a good first officer back at the beginning of j-high. But since his dad died, he's gone totally dube, just when his mom needed him most so I decided he isn't First Officer material.

And so, I say to Brother Number 3, "This list will take a place of honor there." Everybody thought that was cool; they would remember this dinner as the Dinner Where We Made The List of Our Favorite Hot Dishes.

DRAFTING

MAKE A SCALE DRAWING OF AN INTERESTING OBJECT. SHOW AT LEAST THREE VIEWS.

Chimes: After a while, Match Game '74 makes you feel like a loser. It was one thing this summer, when we all sat around wisecracking after playing poker or Monopoly, but once high school started, I was watching it alone. Everyone was all psyched about getting their letter in cross country which, as far as I can tell, meant getting a varsity letter for running painful distances for no apparent purpose. And, of course, Quint King was evidently under the illusion that you could letter in recreational drug use. Dad worked the night shift at the Minnisapa Daily News, which is when the paper was designed and printed; Mom wouldn't be home 'til 5:00 and my little brother went to a friend's house.

So when I found myself eating a peanut butter sandwich and saying "Charles Nelson Reilly, America's Sweetheart" to my mom's dog I realized that, unlike that sissy dog, I needed something other than to be sitting alone in our living room: the TV didn't get me.

But when I turned the TV off, I got smacked with the silence. This neighborhood had never been silent before: now it felt like the day after the Ruskies had dropped a bomb. There had always been sounds in the street and, like most kids, I thought those sounds were as much a part of home as the couch and the curtains. It wasn't like the sounds were idyllic: we were hardly little frolicking shepard's kids. Somebody had usually gotten blasted in the face or started an argument about the true interpretation of tie-goes-to-the runner or was making motorcycle sounds with their sting ray. We were peevish; we screamed like we were being raped; we did stupid things and tripped and bled and sobbed. When it rained, we read superhero comics because they showed the only adults who actually ran around. Our dads were good guys but they stood around and had opinions or poked at flower beds and creaked when they straightened back up.

I decided that I had to get the hell out of the house. So, I said, "See ya, loser" to the dog and walked up to Munson Avenue in the annoyingly cheerful September sunshine. When I got to the high school, I took a deep breath and kept going toward the bowling alley. I'd been there before. Smash and I would show up over the summer, after we'd both rolled 160s in a ninth grade phys-ed class. But this was the first time I went alone. I was just a kid going to a bowling alley but I felt like I was doing something illegal.

I wasn't making the brightest moves. Walking along the street, I looked back behind the school and there were four burn-outs back there and the one with his back to me had long hair and some sort of army jacket like Quint King was favoring these days. He seemed to be toking on something. I was so glad to see him, I yelled, from maybe 100 yards away, "Quint, you fucking hippie."

The guy spun around. He looked like a senior and he yelled, "What's that, asshole? Come over here and say that." and then took off after me.

I took off. I couldn't tell what he was doing until I heard him say, "That's it. Run you little fucking girl."

I strolled into the bowling alley without my usual James

Bond-like composure. In fact, my heart was beating like a rabbit's and I was afraid to pick up my pop.

The gruff old son-of-a-bitch behind the counter, who would normally pre-empt any conversation by asking you, "What size?" when you entered, and then waving a lizardy bowling shoe in your face if you didn't know what he meant, asked, "You okay kid?"

I knew how to play this guy. 'Yeah, got chased by some hippies."

He snorted.

"Hippies got no wind."

He laughed.

My immense self-knowledge can be a burden. I knew who I was. I knew I was a click away from being one of those lonely kids who was kind of good at something so he practiced it by himself, hoping someone would join in. I was a click away from being one of those kids you always thought was a dork and then you saw their picture in the paper for some ballroom dancing or archery triumph and then you saw them beaming in school the next day and you knew they were a dork.

I'd never been that guy before. From the time we learned how to use the phone, or just to walk into the street, I'd be in on a football game or a kickball game or an expedition on bikes and, then, in junior high, Monopoly tournaments and poker games. We'd all gone to Juaire-Manley elementary; we'd all nursed the ancient tribal hatreds toward the kids at Heise-Johnson and Pelowski-Libera. (All elementary schools in Minnisapa are named after two people, so no one gets a big head.) In Troop 15, we'd all terrorized tenderfoots and subsisted on canned frosting and burnt Dinty Moore stew; we'd all snuck peeks at the Playboys at Hubie's Foods. But in high school I was in the particular hell that is life without extracurricular activities. I missed those guys, but the only option seemed to be signing up as a team manager, and I was not about to become a team manager. What the hell would that involve, anyway? Precisely what about a bunch of guys running around requires management? So that left the bowling alley. I knew the owner and some of the older kids who worked the lanes, but it was still a little lame. But lame seemed to be my best option.

"You've got talent, but you don't know what the fuck you're doing." This was how Jimbo Lane—actual name, other than his own upgrading of Jim to Jimbo—began his mentoring. In Minnisapa, adults do not swear at children, at least not in my neighborhood. He looked like a guy who lost a few fights and won a few more. He had a crew cut in 1974. He wore clip-on ties. He looked at my bowling ball and said, "Gimme that damn thing." I did.

He gazed at the bowling ball, as if he considered it my superior, and said, *to the bowling ball,* "Where to fucking start?" He then turned to me and actually said, without irony, "Get a fucking grip" and started to demonstrate the proper way to hold the ball. And I made a note to tell the "get a grip" story to the guys. And then: "Get a fucking ball. You're a skinny ass kid. Stop using fucking Fred Flintstone's ball. Then, we'll work on your stance, your approach, your release, your follow-through. Oh, we'll work on fucking everything there is, Bugs. You're a fucking project. I can see right away, you've got the fucking smirk." Was it that obvious? The smirk that said, *I don't recall asking for any advice and I am, technically, a customer.* Jimbo thought he could read me, but he only knew half of what I was thinking. I was also thinking, "Man, I'll have stories to tell the guys for the next year" and I was also thinking, "Cool, I'm a project."

I sized up Jimbo and thought, "grumpy but lovable" but there was something else going on. Once when I wasn't getting the hang of something, he said, "No, no, no" about eighteen times and the veins in his neck bulged. When I mentioned this to my dad one Saturday over dinner, I learned that Jimbo had been a teacher at the high school years ago and had bounced a kid's head off a drafting table. Maybe a couple of kids. This was back in the 50s. They spotted you a kid or two before they fired you. People who were bad at drafting made him mad. I remember feeling lucky that I was naturally good at bowling.

Drafting and bowling are both things you can get perfect. They are also things that precisely measure what a fuck-up you are. Practicing, with Jimbo looking over at me, I would be in a zone, throwing five, six, seven straight strikes. It was like I was Samantha on *Bewitched*: it was like I blinked and knocked 'em over. Then I would hear the ball hurry back up the ball return, then slow and slide and bump. At this point, even though it's just me, I'm starting to feel the butterfly in my guts and I'm breathing like a bullfrog. Big breaths in, puffed cheeks with the air hissing out my lips, arms noodly, mind empty, eyes so focused they almost burn. I let the air from the little fan in the ball-return cool my hands; I grab my ball, grip it, and bring it up to my chest. I stand where I'm supposed to stand. I stare at the pins like a nun staring at Jesus. Butterflies in the stomach, bullfrog in the cheeks. I shift my vision to the arrows in the lane. I contemplate them. I approach: the same three steps toward the lane, the same release point, the same release. But some damn little hiccup somewhere, something I did for too long or not long enough, some stray thought has sabotaged everything. I know it when the ball leaves my hand. I leave two pins standing. Back behind the counter, Jimbo sees my failure and slams the counter so hard the ashtrays jump.

The girls in my class at school play a game called "Who

Does He Think He Is?" Jimbo thought he was Lou Grant. But Lou Grant wouldn't have slammed that counter.

That said, I always got along with the guy just fine. My dad wasn't crazy like Jimbo but, because he ran the graphics department at the Minnisapa Daily News, I always kept quiet at breakfast while he read the paper. Watching my dad read the paper was like watching an opera. If there was a typo, or an ad was a little crooked, you'd get the "dammit" and a couple minutes of silence with his face in his hands.

With my dad, though, if everything was laid out the way it was supposed to be, he'd fold the paper and say, "That's a thing of beauty." He'd practically cry.

The one thing you never say to guys like that was, "It doesn't matter." With my dad, you'd get the lecture about how societies that excuse shoddiness in philosophy because it's an exalted profession and in plumbing because it's a lowly one wind up with theories and pipes that can't hold water. You only want to hear that lecture once. I didn't want to find out what you'd get from Jimbo if you said, "It doesn't matter."

I loitered my way into a job. Jimbo hired me after one of the older high school guys showed up stoned and then I wound up in a league when my co-worker, the charismatic-only-to-himself Daryl Ewing, wheedled me into joining his team of "Young Turks." Ewing would actually say stuff like, "We are the Young Turks and we are the new face of bowling." After every strike, he had a double-fist pump/knee flex signature move he must have gotten straight off an after-school special about saucy urban youth. He looked like David Cassidy, only much dorkier. He'd say, "Pass the butter 'cause you're toast." He was almost too stupid to hate. Besides me his recruits included Duane Einwald, a kid who just moved in from some farm town where an army jacket and brief case combo was the height of fashion and who we tormented with constantly changing nicknames, and Ricky Zumbro, a college kid who kept talking about health benefits of peach nectar and who actually said once, "My new girlfriend and I are really into our bodies." Being the leader of men that I am, I whipped this ragtag group into a force to be reckoned with in Minnisapa bowling.

I bowled well and, one night, I absolutely caught fire. Eight frames into it, I knew that people were talking about the game I was throwing: eight strikes. After I threw the ninth strike, it was like flash bulbs were suddenly exploding everywhere. I took a crap, just to calm down. When I came out of the john and walked up to take my turn, the whole alley shut down and everyone watched. I was sick to my stomach, but I knew that came with the territory. The guys were solemn and mumbled, "Come on, man, you can do this" and "You've got the power"; it wasn't like cheering; they sounded like gospel preachers on TV when they close their eyes and pep up a cripple. I made sure my hands were dry. I picked up my ball up from the waiting line-up of balls in the absolutely quiet alley. I stood where I always stood. I double-checked that I was standing where I was supposed to be. With the ball at my chest, I looked at the pins until I barely existed. I looked at the arrows on the lane and began my approach. I knew it was perfect when it left my hand, but I had to wait for however long it took the ball to hook into the 1 and 3 pins; I just stored up the celebration in my arms; then everything fell; nothing even wobbled, and I spun and my team was there raising high fives and I swear I high-fived every guy in that alley that night.

The next day, I was afraid I was going to pay for it. I was afraid I was going to become a joke. I was in the paper. Thanks to Dad, the front page. Of course, Burpee was psyched. But then Slow came up to me and shook my hand. Slow's whole world is pretty much built on handshakes. I think he practices them. Even Barb Carimona and Sarah Hamilton congratulated me. Sarah, like she was giving me a retirement watch, but Barb leaned in with her big mane of not-exactly-blonde hair and questioning face and touched me on the forearm, which is a special girl thing.

I just wish I didn't know what I know: we're "nice kids" which means we don't say things to people's faces. Niceness involves a certain amount of bullshit. But then Smash came up to me, grabbed me in a headlock, and said, "Perfection. Good fucking job."

MUSIC

Barb Carimona: Stupid me, I expected high school to be better; I thought the boys and I could maybe relate like normal human beings; but everything's worse: it's like living in a world where people can start playing ping pong in the middle of a conversation. Sometimes I say something that I think is honest and true and normal and one of the boys will ricochet it back at me. I suppose they've always done this, but they seem to hit harder now, with more spin. The boys are not healthy creatures, but I've known them forever and you can't just say to another human being, *you aren't important anymore*. I mean, we played kick ball together in grade school and ditch in junior high. I don't want them to go away. I just want them to be more like my dad and my mom and even my dumb little sister and brother who, despite their many faults, don't spend all their time searching for ways to sting me.

We're sitting in Mr. Huff's class. The boys were making fun of some song. The way they sang it, I thought it must have been a Bob Dylan song. I couldn't make out many of the words but they sang the words "lifetime" and "night time" like they were strangling a cat. But the thing is, they'd all just bought this record, like the minute it came out.

So I said, "If you don't like Bob Dylan, don't buy his records."

Smash said, "What the hell you talking about Barb?"

"That song. Stop making fun of it."

"You think that's a Dylan song?"

"Uh, yes."

"Shows you what you know."

I'm so stupid. I couldn't say anything now. Sarah Hamilton was looking concerned for me. She asked, "Well, so who sings it?"

Smash said, "We're not telling. Barb might ruin it by buying it."

Dickie Burpee, who is just a goofy little thing, was giving a presentation, so Sarah and I decided we didn't really need to pay much attention. It's not like the test would say, "Please discuss the fascinating implications of Dickie Burpee's presentation." So, because we were a little mad at the boys, we were playing "Who Does He Think Is?" We looked at Smash, in his pimp shirt, and Sarah scribbled a note and pushed it toward me: "Burt Reynolds." We looked at Quint King, who had actually shown up today, and I wrote down, "Gregg Allman" and slipped it to Sarah. She wrote back, "Yes, but cuter," which surprised me. We looked at Slow Slocum and I had written down "Robbie, on My Three Sons" and Sarah had written down "Fred MacMurray" and passed it to me, and we'd almost laughed because Slow looks cute but acts like everybody's dad. Sarah won, because the game really isn't about who they happen to look like, but it's easy to get confused. We'd written down "Bill Cosby" for Chimes and Chimes is a skinny blond white guy.

Because we weren't paying much attention to what was

going on, it took us a while to realize that Burpee had messed up. I don't suppose that's all that surprising. But then it became clear that he'd *really* screwed up. Evidently, like halfway through his speech, he'd started saying "war on puberty" when he meant "war on poverty." Everyone laughed at him and then he froze like dog I'd once seen trapped at this intersection where Highway 61 and Munson Avenue and the Collins Frontage and Erickson Street all smush together.

My dad pulled onto the shoulder across from the Happy Chef and tried to coax the poor thing over, but it kept darting away. Cars veered and honked and ruffled the poor dog's hair. A policeman my dad knew showed up and shut down the intersection and he and my Dad rescued that poor little dog.

But when poor Burpee repeated "Lyndon Johnson's War on Puberty" a third time, I couldn't rescue him. I couldn't move or speak. But Sarah tried to whisper "poverty" to Burpee and then Smash just yelled, "It's poverty, dumb-ass." And Burpee said, "That's what I said." Then Mr. Huff stood up and said, "Okay, class, I know it's amusing that Dickie got his terms wrong for a few seconds there, but let's listen quietly to the rest of his presentation. Remember: it's *poverty*, Dickie." Burpee limped through the rest of his presentation and took a deep breath every time he had to say "poverty" and you could tell that he was almost ready to cry but didn't.

That night, Sarah and I went to Kootch's Records, which was less a regular store than a sort of house by the railroad tracks. I didn't tell her that the reason I wanted to buy the record the boys were singing was that *Seventeen* had suggested you should buy the music that boys like.

We were actually frightened. This wasn't our part of

Minnisapa. This was an outpost of the world of boathouses and old Victorian houses where the hippies lived.

"I'm actually kind of scared," I said.

"Oh, come on. It's not like we're doing a drug deal."

"It feels like we are."

She said, "Let's not be such weenies."

I said, "But we are weenies. We are such weenies."

Sarah didn't say anything, but made a face which indicated she agreed with me.

Then, I said, "They might *feed us LSD*. They might sell us into white slavery."

"They might chop us into little pieces and sell us to perverts."

"Or worse," I said and we went on like that for a while. Boys don't realize how irresistible hysteria can be.

But we were a little nervous when we entered the store. The sign was hand painted, with roses and skulls in the letters. Some of the roses poked out of the skull's eyes. The inside was dark, and when I stepped in behind Sarah, a smoky sweet smell practically molested me. At first, I flinched at the music, which came from these speakers the size of bodyguards but then I realized it was the Byrds, who I kind of recognized. I'd never felt music thicken the air in a room like that before. Two hippies leaned over bins and flipped records. Their hair hung over their faces like death hoods. They flipped so slowly that it seemed like they were deciding which souls to take to the underworld with them. Then we glimpsed a case with metal pipes and pinchers and little rectangular golden cases and plastic tubes and turquoise ornaments. We probably spent too long gawking at this, because we could sense the owner walking over to us. Plus, Sarah whispered, "it's practically Sumerian" and since this was a store the size of a living room, everyone probably heard her. But when we looked up, we saw that the owner was a roly-poly man in a silk shirt decorated with elves and he asked in the gentlest kindergarten teacher voice, "Is there anything I can help you with?"

I think Sarah was embarrassed because she'd been heard, so she stepped aside and pretended to browse. So I said, "Yes, I heard this song but I don't have the title or anything."

"Happens all the time. I'll see what I can do."

"It kind of goes . . ." and then I spoke the lines I remembered.

"Yup. Steely Dan. Just released." And then he added, "Under 's'" to be kind.

We had to bump past one of the hippies. We said, "Excuse me" but he seemed put out by our existence. He disliked beings who giggle.

The album cover was a beautiful color photograph, mostly out of focus, with a katydid in the center. The katydid looked vulnerable.

I pointed to it and said, "Dickie Burpee's graduation picture."

Sarah laughed and I felt like a jerk.

As we walked out of the store, into regular air, I said, "I'm still mad at Smash for being so mean."

"You criticized him, Barb. You poked a dog with a stick. Don't be so surprised when he bites you."

Sometimes I think Sarah is a little cynical and that this, more than her legendary intelligence, will serve her well in life.

"No, I didn't poke a dog with a stick. I told a human being that he should act decently."

"Singing a song in a funny voice is an act of indecency?"

"It is in my world," I said and we didn't talk on the way home.

The next day, I was eating my lunch, because I hated the lame, fattening lunch the school provides. I was gnawing my apple and yogurt in peace, like a good little rabbit. I was sitting next to Sarah but talking with the other girls at the table.

The usual madness of the lunchroom had once again become something like a riot, thanks to the orange halves which the grownups had, in their infinite wisdom, served. I got that sense in my shoulders you get when you know boys are throwing things. I could feel the oranges passing behind my back.

Sarah had a better view of the action than I did. She used this as a reason to start talking to me.

"It's okay, Barb. The boys are just laying siege to the Herky Hawk banner."

"But how can you stand it?" I asked because I really wanted the answer. I was about to explode.

"Ignore it," she said. I don't know how you can ignore things and be alive. Don't dead people ignore everything?

"Oh," Sarah reported, "it does appear that the boys are turning on each other."

I heard Chimes Sanborn saying, "Man down, I'm going in!" and then laughter and splats. I couldn't tell how close they were to me. They seemed to be throwing the orange halves really hard.

I asked Sarah, "Where are the grown-ups here?"

"Evidently conferring. I think they're going to let the boys play themselves out."

"Good God," I said. "What cowards."

I couldn't help myself. I turned and yelled, "What are you beasts doing?" Smash Sarnia yelled, "This is not your war!" He smiled. He may have been flirting.

That's when Burpee got the bright idea to yell, "Traitor," which didn't even make sense, and throw an orange half at me. It stung my chest, and dripped onto my boobs. He might as well have vomited on me. The school might as well have vomited on me.

I wanted to die. I started to cry in front of everyone. Sarah put her hand on my back, but even she couldn't think of anything to say that might make it better. I heard Slow Slocum say in his Dad voice, "Jeez, Burpee. Not exactly chivalrous," but that made it worse. I kept sobbing. Sarah walked me to the girl's room and we got most of the stuff out, but my top was wet. I was mortified. She was going to take me to the principal's office to see if I could go home and change. And who's there when we walk out of the bathroom but Burpee, with his head down, and it looks like he's been crying.

"I'm really sorry," he said, and it's pretty clear that he really was. I'm deprived of my one satisfaction, which was hating him.

"That's okay," I said, although I don't know why.

That night, I put *Katy Lied* on and the music was beautiful. Like jazz, but less annoying. I liked the other songs, but sometimes the lyrics ran away from the beauty of the music, as if the lyrics were ashamed of beauty of the music. But I loved "Any World (That I'm Welcome To)" because it was unafraid. I played it over and over again, so much so that I turned the volume down so my mom and dad wouldn't notice anything weird. When I played it, I saw an orange and purple June twilight disappearing through the leafy trees in our neighborhood; I felt the sky become as rich as ink; I saw fireflies blossom in our yards and windows illuminate in our homes; I could feel the presence of the boys, when they were really still boys, sneaking and running and hiding with their hearts beating and their breaths rasping.

I would not tell the boys I had bought this album. I did not want to talk about this with them. They would use it to hurt me.

MAMMALS

TELL WHY ALL MAMMALS DO NOT LIVE IN THE SAME KIND OF HABITAT.

Quint: I could barely stand being in school, what with the jocks, the goody-goody kids, the polyester shirts, plastic pod chairs in the concourse, and the cell blocks of classrooms. The place even smelled phony. Yet I attended a pep rally. I don't know why; I just didn't have the moral fiber not to. A bunch of us stoners—Burpee and Tulep and Bonnie Nether and Kim McCown and I—sat way in the back. 'Cause it was Halloween, there were pumpkins up there with big stupid grins and candles laughing and echoing inside them. We all looked at each other as Principal Pep Rally stood up in front of everybody and got all excited about The Big Game. Tulep says, "I can't deal with this—let's head out. I'll distract Asshole." Asshole was our pet name for the Vice Principal. So Tulep, who can be smooth as hell, slides on over and gets on the other side of Asshole and asks a very involved question and I tap Burpee and we all slide out and sprint to Tulep's car, and then Tulep comes running out, faster than I've ever seen him run, and Burpee opens the door for him but smacks him with it, and Tulep's like, "You fuckin' moron. You could have killed me. You fuckin' moron," and I tense up at this nasty side of Tulep that everyone else seems used to and I'm like, "It's just Burpee, man. It's just

Burpee. Let's ride." Burpee is harmless. Burpee's whole family is harmless; they're dumb as rocks but they're harmless. His mom served us hot cocoa in July and she didn't even notice how stoned we all were; she was so happy that Dickie was bringing over his friends. On the other hand, Tulep can be an angry fuck, but he's got a lot of shit going on, so we cut him slack. Bonnie slides a big ol' bag of pot out of her coat and Tulep says, "There should be some Southern under the seat, but you guys gotta fucking chip in." So we drink the Southern and smoke the dope, and both Bonnie and Kim lean in close to me so we can share the bottle and the joint. We are amazed at what we pulled off. I figure it's a good idea to calm down Tulep, so I say, "It was amazing the way you played Asshole there. That was sweet," and Tulep said, "Yeah, he didn't know what hit 'em." And then I was holding the Southern and raised it in a toast and said, "Here's to Principal Pep Rally" and everybody said, "Here's to Principal Pep Rally," and then Kim started laughing because she always starts these hysterical cackly witchy laughing things like the minute she takes a toke, and she keeps laughing and laughing and we say, "What's so funny," and "Way to be into it," but she doesn't ever stop and she starts to both cry and laugh. I say, "You okay?" and she catches her breath and she's like, "I'm fine; it's nothing; it's just this weird thing I do; I think I've got like pot asthma," and she keeps laughing and crying and saying it's nothing. and Burpee starts riffing on how he's gonna try to get his mom to write him a note saying he has pot asthma, and Tulep says, "Burpee, your mom can't fucking write," and by this time I'm finally starting to catch a buzz like somebody stuck some saxophone-solo and sunlight in my head, and then we're on the bridge over to Wisconsin and the bridge always puts a sad, tickly feeling in my gut. Then Tulep pulls his beater car into the gravel parking lot of this bar that actually looks like a trailer home by the river and we all pile out and when we step in, the darkness of the bar freaks us out, but we try to stay cool and not stumble, and when we can finally make out the faces, it's like three old people and this bartender we know, who I think might be fucking Kim, which is why we're getting served here, and it's still so strange and dark that the neon beer signs are like those fish that glow in the caverns of the ocean and the old people at the bar sway like seaweed and we drift over to a table where I say, "I copped some cash from my mom's dresser," so the consensus is that I'm buying. When I turn around to walk up to the bar, this *monster's face* pierces and pokes at me, and I yell, "What the fuck is that!?" And then the monster spins its head and there's another face on the back of it's head but this time it's a horrible old lady face, all wrinkled and pouchy and pale, and she says, "I didn't mean to scare you, honey; it's just that my trick or treat mask got in the way of my drinking," and everybody cracks up at how freaked out I got. There's this rubber band that runs across her forehead like a string of snot. The asshole bartender says, "I didn't mean to scare you, *honey*," when he slides me the pitcher and I play along, 'cause I'm no dummy, but I now fucking hate this guy and for some reason this moment reminds me of something that happened last week at one of these middle-of-the-day things where a bunch of us wound up at a boat house and I started making out with this girl and she told me to meet her at her place the next afternoon and I did and, it was weird, it felt like I was going to a doctor's office to get a shot, only I was getting fucked; I showed up with a sick feeling in my gut and she nodded when I got there and we started to do it right away because she seemed too nervous to do anything else and the place smelled odd, like the dishes hadn't been washed in quite a while, and the carpet was like greasy poodle hair, and afterwards, when she lay there with her head across my chest, and she loosened up a little, I said, "It's nice to be somewhere where you can move without fear of breaking something," and she said

"Oh, Quint, nobody cares much about that around here," which gave me another sick feeling in the pit of my stomach, and we sat there and she talked about how her uncle was a jerk and how she hated school and how she'd moved here a couple of months ago after something happened to her mom and she talked again about how she hated her uncle. We lay there for like another two hours and watched stupid TV, the kind of shows that make you feel like you're sniffing glue, and we drank and smoked dope. I learned that her uncle kept her supplied with booze and dope.

And the more I thought about that, as I was sitting in that sad dark bar in the morning, the madder I got, until I decided to ask if anybody has seen her and Tulep said, "She high-tailed it to South Dakota or someplace," and I didn't say anything but I knew I had to be alone.

So I buy another pitcher, so people won't follow me, and I leave the bar and nearly fall over 'cause the sunlight is so damn bright it practically tackles you and I start to walk back across the bridge. I look down into the water that moves like sadness and at the trees which are brown like loss and the sky that's empty like grief and I light a cigarette and let the match fall and helicopter like a maple seed and watch the match fall asleep in the water and I let the booze and the dope and the smoke sweeten my sadness and I think of slipping over the bridge and letting myself fall into the river and that sick feeling comes back into my stomach. Then I start walking home and when I get there I will find the bottle of Yukon Jack I've hidden and I will try to ignore the Hummel figurines who spy on me from every buffet and bureau and I will turn on the stereo, the Allman Brothers, *Live at the Fillmore East*, and I will play an imaginary guitar on an imaginary stage and the music will wail and excavate something that nothing else can touch and I will less dance than dervish and I will think of how that girl was beautiful in a stemmy, stalky way I'm afraid she will never recognize and I know that I will never speak to her again and that I can ask and ask about her but I will never get an answer and that God is such a fucking mediocrity and a cheat and that God could have made a passionate cascading universe and he fucking didn't and, then, I will leave the house when I have no more whiskey and I will walk and walk and walk. Unlike God, I will make an unambiguous gesture. You will know that I exist, and you will deal with me.

CRIME PREVENTION

VISIT A JAIL OR DETENTION FACILITY

Quint: I could see the flashing lights, even though they were behind me; the night was all infused with red and panic and yelping, so I knew that I was screwed.

"You. Stop."

"Is there a problem, sir?"

"'Is there a problem, sir?' Yeah. There's a problem. You just threw a rock through someone's window. You could have killed someone."

"—." I wanted to say something but nothing came out.

"Hold still while I put these on. Get in the car."

"Yes, sir."

"You understand that you're in serious trouble."

"Yes, sir. I certainly do."

"No, I don't think you do. I don't think that you realize that you could have killed someone."

"Yes, sir."

"You did substantial property damage, and you could have killed someone."

"Yes, sir."

"You understand that?"

"Yes, sir."

"I don't think you do."

"Yes, sir. I'm very sorry, sir."

"The flashing lights and the handcuffs kind of make it real, don't they?"

"Yes, sir. They do."

"You're Henry King's boy, aren't you? I knew your father. I was in the Knights of Columbus with him. Do you think he'd be proud?"

"No, sir. I don't think so."

"Hi there, Bobby. This is Barney and Andy and we're bringing in John Dillinger. Yeah. You might want to have an extra box of Kleenex on hand. When we mentioned Dillinger's Dad, we kinda opened the floodgates. Yeah. He can't stop crying."

PERSONAL FITNESS

EXPLAIN TO YOUR MERIT BADGE COUNSELOR VERBALLY OR IN WRITING WHAT PERSONAL FITNESS MEANS TO YOU, INCLUDING WHAT YOU CAN DO TO PREVENT SOCIAL, EMOTIONAL, OR MENTAL PROBLEMS.

Slow: We were sitting around in Bridgeman's, which is the local ice-cream parlor, and which is as far away from the boathouses where dope fiends like Quint King party as it is possible to be and still be in Minnisapa. If you wanted to get any farther away, you'd have to transport yourself into an Archies comic book, which would be cool, but which is still technologically impossible. I had ordered a lime phosphate, mainly because "phosphate" sounds cool; Pooch had the peppermint bonbon sundae, because he's always trying to bulk up to make up for the year he missed when he skipped sixth grade. We had some sheets of that sort of beige graph paper with light blue lines that we like. We were making a list of people we thought were level-headed.

We'd just played an intramural b-ball game—we're both varsity in cross-country and track—and felt pretty good. Our team, which is the only team in the entire league with a decent name, had just beaten Kelly's Killers—see what I mean about the names?—even though we had a bad game. The Killers, which they kept calling themselves in their simian way, kept trying to do these incredibly j-high reverse layups—where you start doing a regular layup and then take the ball under the net and up—and missing them. Which just goes to show how important discipline is. One of those clowns actually turned and smacked himself on the chest with both fists after he missed a shot, just because he'd knocked Pooch on his ass and shook the backboard. Pooch, who had shown great resilience by hustling back on offense to hit a jumper, said that "until somebody actually eats a banana on court while scratching their ass, that's the most simian moment any of us are ever going to witness."

Our team is called Death Before Dishonor. It is the greatest name for an intramural team of all time because the whole point is that I.M. isn't all serious and rah rah and character building like varsity sports. We all have shirts with Death Before Dishonor on the front and, instead of our names, our favorite violation on the back. For example, Smash is called "Technical Foul." Pooch is "Traveling" because he's fast but he dribbles like a dube.

A couple of weeks before, we'd sat around Pooch's room, which is this huge basement room with a john in one corner and made a list of people from our school who we thought might, upon graduation, become serial killers. We had to use the yearbook for that one, because they weren't—kind of by definition—guys we would hang out with. Surprisingly, none of the football players made the serial-killer list. We figured they'd smack you around in their simian problem-solving way but they wouldn't wipe out a whole McDonald's or anything. Why is Mac and Don's such a nut magnet? Why don't any of these psychos go ballistic in Burger King? We didn't even think hoods like Tulep would go serial killer; they'd just knock you off when they were sticking up a SuperAmerica.

Pooch and I and our whole crowd are big on lists. We'll sit around in the concourse, now that we don't have C.C. practice after school, and make lists of ridiculous stuff or just generally discourse on the absurdity of life. We make up fake top 40s. Songs like "Party Every Third Night" by the Incinerator Boys. The joke there is that some lame band, seeing all those songs about Partying Every Night, thinks that they just might have a chance if they talk about Partying Every *Third* Night.

But we make our serious lists off-site. There was a list of the top twenty-five babes in each class, which we'd made at Pooch's. We'd heard that some of the basketball players, who are borderline simian and dope fiend but who we still know to say hi to because they're on student council and stuff, had made a list, but when we finally procured a copy, it was just a list of girls with a ranking of one through ten next to their name based on what these four guys had said.

Statistically, it wasn't very sophisticated. We broadened the pool to a dozen guys and instituted a couple of improvements: first, a 1—100 scale for more fine discrimination; then, three separate scores—one for body, one for face, and one for personality, although personality usually correlated pretty closely to looks, so it was really just a tie breaker; and, finally, at Pooch's suggestion, we dropped the high and low score for every girl in every category, to make it all more statistically valid.

We showed that list to the basketball guys, and they were duly impressed because some of them are in pre-calc, or at least trig, so they could appreciate our statistical rigor, but, besides that, we kept it under wraps. You can't resist doing this kind of stuff, but you also know that, if it got out, somebody's feelings might get hurt. I do know that some girls did circulate their own ranking because they heard about the basketball guys' one and got mad, but I was fourth out of 272 guys, so I didn't mind that too much. The top three were unreliable guys like my dad, so fourth was okay.

The list of level-headed people was proceeding pretty well, but the fuel was running out. If I drank any more of my phosphate through my straw, I'd make those slurping noises, and Pooch was smacking the bottom of his sundae to dislodge some ice cream/fudge alloy. We decided to order dinner and keep working. I had the steak sandwich. He had the chicken sandwich with an extra order of fries. I think it's safe to say that a Spirit of Free Inquiry prevailed. We put a couple of liberals on our list and one chick. We nixed some of our friends because, while they were our friends, they weren't really level-headed.

"Smash is off," I said, although I actually thought Smash was more level-headed than he seemed.

"Well, yeah," Pooch said, as if I'd started a pre-calc problem by verifying two plus two.

"Because of his name?" I said.

"Because he devotes his life to living up to it. Because he told Barb Carimona and Sarah Hamilton that he would take his mom to prom if the girls in our class didn't stop being such losers. Because when that call went against him tonight, he hung from the climbing rope and banged against the gym wall and wailed."

"But I think we have to define our criteria here, Pooch. He was just pissed. But basically Smash has a good head on his shoulders."

"Which he *beats against walls*."

"But I think the criteria here should be: would they join a cult? Smash would never join a cult." This went back to a theory I'd thought of this last summer, when I'd stayed in Connecticut with my dad.

"He'd probably start one," Pooch kind of snorted.

And then we spent some time elaborating on what Smash's cult would be like. How, for their initiation, new members would have to take a basketball and bounce it off a wall so hard it bounced back and knocked them out, which Smash actually did once. We ate for a while, and I ordered some more fries.

"Man, a lot of guys who I thought in j-high were pretty level-headed have surprised me," I said.

"Quint King whipped a brick through a window last night. Shattered like two-thousand dollars' worth of Hummel figurines. And he was, like, Joe Level-Headed in J-High." We silently pondered Quint's fall, and then I asked Pooch if I could finish his fries.

Last summer, when I was living with my dad in Connecticut, all the kids I met seemed like ripe candidates for the Krishnas. My parents divorced about five years ago, so my dad moved away to be a big executive and left Mom with the six of us in Minnisapa. I've tried my best to be the man of the house, especially since my dad had been such a jerk, although I'm gone a lot for sports. I didn't get a lot of details, 'cause I was just in j-high. I do know that my mom blew her nose a lot in her room, and when she came out, she had that look you get when you talk to a priest, and that my dad was gone a lot on business but that I saw him once at McDonald's, and he pretended not to see me and sort of prayed into his Big Mac, and a couple of times I made Hamburger Helper for everybody because Mom had never even bothered to come out of my parents' room, and I may not be as smart as Pooch but I'm not stupid.

In his new job in Connecticut, my dad worked in the day, and a lot of evenings, so I had time to myself. I tried to make friends with the local kids. A lot of these kids had divorced parents, and they seemed both harder and more vulnerable than Minnisapa kids. They made fun of sports, and nobody was interested in science or math, and they all just sort of hung around these fancy houses, which were set back in pine trees on twisty roads like it was a huge summer camp or something. They all had rich-people stuff like intercoms and picture windows and breakfast nooks and conversation pits, which were really TV pits.

Those Connecticut kids would have thought the kind of stuff we did in Minnisapa was stupid. For example: Once we got twenty guys in a double-elimination Monopoly tournament that lasted pretty much all summer. Or else we would sit around and fill out a presidential cabinet with our friends—we'd do weird stuff, like make Chimes Sanborn secretary of bowling. Most times I'd be secretary of state because I'm good at talking to grown-ups. We'd make Smash secretary of labor because he swore a lot. Or else Pooch and I would just sit around after running and compare resting pulses and eat Neapolitan ice-cream sandwiches and talk about things like, "What kind of houses did Frank Lloyd Wright draw when he was a little kid when the teachers made him draw a house, and did he get into trouble for not drawing a box with an A on top of it like everybody else?"

These Connecticut kids didn't do any of that stuff. They snuck their parents' booze and smoked dope and watched soap operas and made jokes about how everything is bogus. They all talked about sex in that way that makes you think they want to suggest something; there was something greasy about the way the words hung there.

Once, that summer in Connecticut, there were five of us hanging out: This neighbor guy who talked a lot and his quiet friend and two girls they knew. One of the girls, who was good-looking in kind of a rough-trade way, was the guys' age and the other was, like, fifteen. Everybody else was passing around a bong, which looked like some sort of eastern sitar love-instrument, and which they leaned over and fiddled with all the time. They all talked and held their breath when they inhaled; when they exhaled, they smiled and talked like they were floating on their backs. "You sure you don't want some, Minnesota," the neighbor guy said.

"No, I'm cool," I said, and felt like a dork for saying "I'm cool" in that, well, I-smoke-a-lot-but-dude-this-afternoon-I'm-just-laying-off-a-little kind of way.

"More for me," he said, and that was pretty much their whole attitude.

And they were all telling stories about different people who sniffed different household compounds and things back in j-high before people could get proper dope and how these activities all permanently damaged some people's brains so dope should really be legal. And then they got more stoned, like they were sleepwalking, and I might as well have been wearing my old Boy Scout uniform with the khaki shorts and the kerchief, and the louder, jerkier guy said, "I bet there's some porn around here."

And even though it wasn't his house, but the house of the vaguely j-high girl, he started searching the parents' bedroom, which had the cologney smell of rich adults' bedrooms, and the other people followed him in, and I said, "Should we really be in here?" which they just ignored, and I started to get sick to my stomach. They started looking through drawers and making fun of the girl's dad's socks, which had various executive-type squiggles on them, and then she said, "Come on, you guys, I'll get in trouble" but they ignored her, and the two of us kind of looked at each other, and she was kind of cute and I thought I should do something chivalrous but I couldn't think of what that might be.

Then jerk guy said, "Check this out," and pulled out a bunch of *Penthouses* and a dildo, which was realistic if the size of my forearm is realistic, and I did say, "There are ladies present, maybe we should cool it a little," but I didn't say it hard enough and this guy in this druggy voice jokes, "All the more reason," and his buddy and the other girl laugh, and the j-high girl looks at me for help but I don't know what to do to help her. But then the rough-trade girl said "Come on, needledick," which got that guy to shut up suspiciously fast. Then she grabbed the dildo and put it away like it was just a baseball glove or something. The guy let her but he kept the *Penthouses*. I wasn't entirely displeased about that.

Back in the conversation pit, the talks-a-lot guy was gawking at one of the pictorials, which was of this guy dressed up—for a while—as a British soldier and these two girls dressed up—for a while—as Colonial maidens, because it was the bicentennial issue, and the guy said, "Now this is what I call the American Dream." And he handed it to the quiet guy who said, "Whoa," and handed it back to him but then loud guy told the quiet guy to pass it on to the quiet girl, so he sheepishly did, and I thought the quiet guy might be okay but weak. The j-high-ish girl didn't quite know where to look, and I felt like a chump because I wasn't doing anything, and then the rough-trade girl grabbed it and said, "Let's see this thing," and looked at it and turned to me and said, "You want a look?" and sort of asked me, "Are you going to help me out and say 'No'?" with her eyes so I shook my head *No* so she quick showed me one page as a kind of reward, and there were these two gorgeous girls naked and kissing each other. I almost shot it right there. I couldn't move for about half an hour.

The door of Bridgeman's opened and we heard, "Sorry, old guy!" Smash appeared from behind some confused senior citizens and popped into our booth. He was wearing this preposterous striped fake-fur coat that went down to his ankles. Pooch and I wore regular down jackets because it was too cold to wear our letter jackets.

While we were exchanging "Berfs"—it kind of means "brother" so we all say it to each other when we first meet—Pooch and I panicked and I tried to flip over the list of level-headed people. Smash, who could tell we'd tried to hide something, picked it up and said, "What the hell's this?"

For some reason, I was embarrassed about it, and my heart was beating hard and I just looked at him. But Pooch improvised, "It's a list of people who would be good for starting a colony on Mars."

Smash said, "You don't want me on Mars?"

I said, "We're not done yet," which I thought was diplomatic. But Pooch said, at the same time, "You're already there, pal."

Smash said, "Fuck you" but, although I'm not huge on swearing, it was that kind of between-guys fuck you that means, "Yeah, whatever."

Then Smash looked the list over again and said, "You're gonna need more chicks," and gave it back to us.

Later that summer in Connecticut, when I was in my dad's house alone, feeling homesick, with the air-conditioner hum vibrating in my marrow, and the leather couch feeling sticky and puffy like some sort of creepy space creature, and the television's color vibrating in my eyes like radiation, I started making a list so secret that not even Pooch knows about it. His dad, who looks like every narrator on every 1950s science film ever made, was on it. Our calc teacher, who says that we talk like dubes and insists that we use the Queen's English in class, was on it. Our cross-country coach, who always runs with us to lead by example, and almost never raises his voice, was on it. It was a list of guys who would make a better dad than the son of a bitch I got. When I got done making it, I ran for miles and miles on those Martian cul-de-sacs, and I didn't care that I didn't know where I was going or that I might not ever find my way back.

ARCHERY

EXPLAIN THE ARCHERY SAFETY RULES

Quint: All day long, everything would happen over and over: It would be nighttime again and I would be walking down the street and then everything shivered and surged like music, and I threw the brick, and the window shattered, and the siren and the flashers made everything all roboty, and the cop grabbed my hands and clicked on the cuffs. All day, this scene would wash over me. Over me? Through me, under me, around me.

Other people have drug flashbacks. I have reality flashbacks.

Finally, the shakiness began to rinse away during the last few minutes of study hall. I'd stayed in the building. Don't know why. And I wandered over to a table with Barb Carimona and some of her friends, because the people I hang around with lately don't spend much time in study hall, so I thought my best bet was to sidle up to these girls I knew from grade school and junior high.

"Barb, how ya doing?"

"Oh, hi, Quint." I tried to tell myself that she wasn't alarmed at the looming presence of a stoner.

As I'm standing there, wanting the drug and eloquence of a cigarette, but instead standing there like Wally Cleaver himself, only less socially assured, this girl named Sarah, who I kind of remembered from Huff's class, appeared. Barb and everybody turned to her.

She stopped at their table like a politician. I had nowhere better to go, so I stood on the edges and watched everything. She was talking about some meeting she was going to where she was the only non-adult.

"And, of course, I will represent the perspective of the Youth of Today."

The way she spoke reminded me of pencil drawings, it was all incisive and innocent like that, with little cross-hatchings and fluencies.

"How was the big college trip?"

"Oh, it was great. New York was scary but I loved it, even though my dad did his best to make it seem as much like a night in Minnisapa as possible. I made him go to an art film with me. He kept saying, 'Sarah, we're such bohemians.'"

She hugged her books and shifted some from hip to hip, like she was used to being in motion, and I swear she looked over at me a couple of times. She wore glasses, and they made her eyes look like water drops blown sideways. She was freckled, and the freckles were like water drops blown sideways, too.

"I really should go and introduce myself to the muckety-mucks, but I wanna tell you guys about this seminar I sat in on."

The seminar was about Zeno's paradox. She explained the paradox: "It's like this: this ancient Greek argued that an arrow can never reach a target because before reaching the target it has to reach a point halfway to the target; then it has to reach a point three-fourths of the way to the target; and then a point seven-eighths of the way there and so on. So no matter how far the arrow moves toward the target, a fraction of distance will still remain. It's supposed to test our little provincial brains."

When I heard this, I blurted out, like an idiot: "So why not just aim a foot behind the target?" I'd been trying to be funny.

She just squinted at me, baffled. Then she said to Barb, "You gotta admire the moxie of a guy who says 'that arrow you just shot never actually reached the target. And I can *prove* it.'" Then she went off to her meeting.

Barb turned to me and said, "Our new favorite word is 'moxie.'"

I said, "I could use some of that. Man, I'm sorry to have just . . . oh, I don't know . . ." The thought just evaporated.

"How ya doing, Quint?" she said in that way that girls have when they actually want to know, but I thought, *Not now, sweetheart, don't ask me that now.*

"Oh, you know how it goes," I said.

"Yeah," she said. And she didn't, but she was being nice.

"I gotta go," I said, and shot out of there like an arrow.

As I left, I couldn't help but look out at the swampy end of Lake Minnisapa and the cattails which were barely plants—what fucking kind of plant is always brown?—and the water which was barely water and I thought that even the lake can't get it together and I fired up a cigarette the moment I left the building and for a minute there my mind was like a saxophone and everything was cool.

As I walked the streets I'd known all my life, I couldn't help but think that Zeno's paradox was uncomfortably autobiographical. Our family had taken trips when I was a kid—a couple of uncomfortable car trips and a lot of train trips, because my dad did a lot of legal work for the railroad. But they seemed like those trips in movies where the backdrops move but the people stay still. And for all of high school I'd been stuck here with my mom, like one of those dreams where you know you have to wake but you can't and you just keep getting more and more scared.

The weather wasn't helping. It had rained all October and everything was brown and grey, and the leaves had been slapped down on the sidewalks. Everything was damp. The fucking dampness was damp and the brown was brown. The weather was like me, only more so. The weather needed some counseling. The weather had to think about the consequences of its actions. I kicked the wet leaves and riffed through the paradox in my mind: 1/2, 3/4, 7/8, 15/16, 31/32, that arrow always shivering in front of its target. If this were only true, I thought. If only it were true.

I decided not to think about Sarah anymore.

The other reason we didn't take family vacations anymore is that we weren't a family anymore. Reasonable enough, I guess. My dad had drowned and my brother and sister had gone away to schools in the Cities. My brother was in med school; my sister was in law school.

This left me and my mom, who was standing there doing dishes when I came in.

"How you doing?" I asked, although I regretted it. I grabbed a cookie and dunked it in some milk and then held it up so a part of it detached into my mouth.

"I'm tired," my mom said, "I had very long day." She was tired because she had had to come down to the police station to get me last night. She focused on the dishes, making a signature of shining blue dishwashing liquid on the sponge. She had just worked a full day as a nurse, too. She was still disappointed in me and wouldn't look me in the eye but stared into the dishwater. I can't say I blame her. Unlike me, the dishes would be like-new in a few minutes.

I set my glass next to the sink and said, "I'm going to go see Dickie Burpee." I didn't tell her that he was housesitting for his grandmother, and that we would be drinking and smoking dope. I'm no dummy.

"Good," she said, "I'm going to sit in the living room and put my feet up." She added, staring out the window: "And take off my shoes." She spent most of her time in the front part of the house, with the Hummel figurines and Catholic icons and the graduation pictures of my more successful siblings. My room was now behind the kitchen. We'd closed off the upstairs rooms; they were like a museum of the days when we were happy: those forty-fives with purple or tangerine or rainbow-colored labels, booklets with names like "Your Child's Progress through the Sacraments," wastebaskets with the faces of 1960s sitcom stars, candles that bled over wine bottles, these paint-by-number oil paintings of dogs that my older brother and sister had done once. As I left, I could see mom shift her weight and lean against the counter, so that she eased the pressure on one foot.

As you might expect, Burpee's grandmother's house was trippy in a grandmother's house kind of way and also in a Burpee kind of way. It pressed in like a hug from an old lady. Ghosty beige curtains. Console stereo with about five polka albums and one Glenn Miller that actually had some decent shit on it, if you just listened to the parts, but Burpee wasn't interested. He had brought his own albums, the usual stoner stuff. There was darkness outside, like outer space had snuck up on the house when we weren't looking. We turned the TV on but kept the sound off and cranked up the records. Hogan's Heroes was on and it was even weirder when it was silent. A family of ceramic puppies stared at me.

Burpee had claimed the dope was laced. He speculated about opium.

I contemplated the dogs and held out the pipe for Burpee to

take. He said, "Thanks, man" and I could feel the pipe being lifted from my hand. I left my hand hang there, then jerked it back to my body. My mind butterflied; it bounced and danced and alighted.

Burpee took a toke and said, "Green," which is weird even for Burpee. I let it percolate, though. The thing that hit my ear wasn't really "green." More Gr-*eee*-EN. Then I tried to figure out if Burpee had inserted these changes, or if they were already in the word, or if they were hidden and he had somehow italicized them but I thought that was beyond Burpee who was probably just dreaming of the Packers. And then the whole problem of "green" started to bang around in my head like a ping-pong ball in a phone booth: After all, it was one word and presumably just one thing but there were, first of all, all those synonyms—all those emeralds, mosses, kellys, limes, forests and then the underground synonyms like snot and swamp and gangrene and those were just summaries and approximations of the different rays of light striking all the surfaces and entering all the eyes and registering in all the brains now and throughout history, an infinity of shadings, an infinity of infinities, each different, all of which we just grunt and call "green" and then when you do say "green" the word itself—you know, the actual sounds you make with your sad particular mouth—it's always different, based on, I don't know, the exact pauses and lubrications, the particular intake and out-rush of air, the configuration of your larynx, the microscopic empires thriving in your throat, whether you've got a cigarette or a Bic pen cap stuck in your mouth, or whether you're chewing Oscar Mayer baloney and saying "green," and who can forget the specific humidity of the air, the freaky presence of invisible radio waves and television emissions which mingle with everything we say. Every word is a billion billion words. We're all just prisoners tapping a code that means something entirely different to each of us. My mind was sax whimper and starry sadness.

And then, on the TV: The birdy oily Nazi prison camp commandant was making these greasy bowing gestures in front of a higher-ranking slow-eyed bulldogish Nazi officer, while the leader of the American POWs smirked.

I'd hit that point where thought just gives way to vibration. Everything trembled. Beer cans, crushed or dusted. Eachly. Very eachly. Is that a word? Those staring basset hounds. There was a plate of fries in front of me with gravy on it.

Finally, I brayed, "Greee-on." And the word broke and fizzled in the room. The word just kept getting weirder.

"Packer green," Burpee declaimed.

"Pecker green."

"Gree-a-oo-n," Burpee said, and started to laugh.

"Grin."

"Gray-on."

"The word is the bird," I said. "The word is the ultimate deluxey deluxe bird."

"What?" asked Burpee. He'd cranked the music. He couldn't hear me. Or maybe I hadn't said anything. I couldn't remember.

I pushed back into the recliner and closed my eyes, because it seemed the thing to do. And of course that's when I started to think about Sarah again, even though I'd decided not to think about her anymore, because even I knew it was a dead-end. But these images of her face kept visiting me like angels, and I would see her freckles which were like a map of how to touch her face, and hear her voice which was as intelligent and gentle as the movement of vision across a page. She was at home, with her parents, studying in clean white light. She wasn't floating in the nasty aquarium of my mind.

This fucking scared me. I'm not unromantic, but my usual

thoughts about girls ran along the lines of "It looks like we're going to wind up together tonight." The romantic stuff came after the sex, not before it, if it came at all. But this was different; it made me nervous. I thought more of these damn not-quite-mine thoughts: What, precisely, is it that exists and moves in her eyes? And why do I need that?

This always happens when I smoke dope. My thoughts froth like one of those buckets full of minnows; my thoughts slip and splash and scare me, and I spend all night trying to calm them down. I heard a chopping which I figured was laughter and which I figured must have come from Burpee but I wasn't quite sure that he existed. How could I prove that other people existed? I mean really prove it and not just hope that they weren't just some dreams that God had projected into my head because he wanted to mess with me. Or that there wasn't even a God but some random projection neuron that ran this constant movie called existence and I was floating somewhere in an icky nothing. The vibration in my mind, the one that felt like an electric fan at the top of my spine, snickered and I couldn't stop it. The skeleton inside me snickered. I looked out from my eyes, from within my skull, from within my mind which was as arrogant as a universe. My mind would make an awful fucking universe. Would make a C- universe. *Please stop this*. If there is a God, he's a prick. I looked out from—and it seemed a real place, a kind of fishing bobber behind my eyes—my consciousness of my consciousness, and my consciousness of my consciousness of my consciousness, and my consciousness of this like infinite nest of self-consciousness from which I could never escape. *Please stop this*. I pressed back into the couch, like an astronaut slammed back into the capsule. But the porcelain dog kept staring and staring and staring, and the cold gravy globs and bent beer cans and the tiny amputations of cigarette butts kept pressing into my eyes, too.

Fuck. An hour had passed.

A disruption in the air that reminded me of Burpee and which may have come from him, disguised as a kitchen. "I'm going to crash here pretty soon, pal. You can stay or listen to tunes or whatever."

Some more time passed. "I'm going to head out," I mumbled, shivering and shaking and waking up.

I didn't hear anything. Burpee must be passed out. So I picked myself up but the world smacked me like an ocean and I tumbled back into the couch. The basset hound stared straight ahead. Its porcelain shone and stared and the light on it looked all buttery, but it had no snicker or sympathy in its sad molecules, it was just something that someone had crafted into the appearance of a being. People should not craft things into the appearance of beings without giving them souls or hope. I stared back at it and then smashed it. The fragments stared at me.

Me and my Molotov mind.

I got up and stumbled toward the door. I couldn't deal with turning off the TV or stereo.

I—if that's the word—lurched outside and the trees felt like darknesses and the darkness felt like trees and everything felt like a grave, like that crumbly earth and those loitering worms, and the cold air percolated and I could go anywhere and do anything and I walked up the street like someone walking through water and the leaves snickered like snakes below me and I walked like Frankenstein, all stiff-kneed and simmering, and the trees dripped like butlers.

I stopped to stop the snakes of the leaves.

And then I let the pictures of Sarah's face arrive, and I felt like that time when I was walking down by the river and the fluttering orange leaves became butterflies, dozens of them, and they scared me until I realized what they were and they still scared me a little even then but they swirled around me like happiness.

But then, I thought, *no, you cannot think these butterfly thoughts*, they will kill you. And I stopped thinking them.

I leaned against a tree. Its bark, like a skin of scars, with its ruts and roughnesses, scraped me. Then, from the past century of this afternoon: Zeno. Something still separates my hand from the tree. How many fractions of an inch?

1/129th? 1/253rd? I gripped it harder, with both hands. The wet bark was rough but still slippery. How close now? I thought. My hands slipped and the tree slapped my face. A house light went on.

I stayed still and got smart. Had I committed a crime? Was this insane? I held still for as long as I could, but I had no idea of time. I tried to count to myself, but I couldn't pace my voice. The numbers quickened then slowed. My clothes were getting wet. I kept making noises. A breath. A movement. A relaxation. Or a tightening. Everything would disturb a thousand leaves. I thought my face hurt, but I couldn't be sure. What was "hurt?" Little ambassadors in my skin were remarking on something that had happened to it. As I tried to lie still, wet leaves tickled my face then covered my mouth.

I got up.

I got up because sometimes you just gotta do the most plausible thing. I got up because lying there with leaves in my mouth didn't really seem an option. Even in this crazy hereness and nowness.

But I walked implausibly, in tune with my cartoon mind, my marching band mind. There was some kind of polka in my cells that I tried to ignore but I couldn't. So I just kept walking past the sane houses.

The light was on. My mom was awake.

I crept into the kitchen, praying *polka soul become cat soul*, and glided past the moment of my mother in the blue light of the campfire of the TV and said, "Good night" in a way that didn't seem too weird and I was almost in my room when I heard the words, "What in the world happened to you? Is that blood on your face?" which had been sent to me from my mother. I'd forgotten about falling into the tree.

"I'm fine. I just tripped playing football."

I was gonna have to wash my face. So I slowly walked toward the bathroom and flipped on the light, which hit me like detergent in the eyes. When I recovered, a monster face scared me. Then was me. Blood-smeared, dirt-smeared, leaf-decoupaged. The bathroom divided into an encyclopedia of a bathroom. The light was like a doctor. I turned the clear plastic knob. I heard the water gush out, all hysterical. I closed the door which made a quick small prison. The water was still hysterical in the sink. It slowed and pooled in my hands. I splashed it on my face. I picked out a washcloth from the origami of washcloths on the rack. The beautiful washcloth became ugly when it touched me. I picked out a towel and breathed in its white cilia and dervished myself dry. I sat down on the toilet seat and pressed the towel to my face to block out the light. *No. Please stop this. Please help me.* It was quiet and calm but I eventually had to leave. I planned. I would have to pass her line of vision, and this time she would be expecting me. I tried to think of what might betray me—some

Charlie Chaplin moment or move.

But sometimes you just gotta do it. I left the bathroom and stared straight ahead as I walked. I heard my mother say something. I knew that her voice was not her, but a vibration of molecules in the air between us.

I heard, "You didn't trip playing football."

The voice was a breeze but the words were a wind. When I escaped to my room, her words followed and, I swear, slammed the door behind me.

That was the only punishment she could exact: to remind me that I was as lonely as an encyclopedia entry, to remind me that all our talk was just a louder silence. I could feel her becoming smaller and scareder and madder in her chair by the campfire of the TV. No longer pretending, I stumbled and surged over everything that littered the floor of my room and I intersected my bed in the giggling trampoliney world. I shut out the light and smashed my covers up to my chin. I lay there, underneath the quilt, staring up at the joke ceiling. It began to snicker and spin. And I knew that everything was made of millions of atoms and those atoms were made of billions of electrons, protons, and neutrons, and none of those billions of particles ever touched another.

INDIAN LORE

Learn 25 Indian place names. Tell their origins and meanings.

Barb Carimona: While people are sitting around a bonfire at the Hamilton's, I announce, "Sarah and I found out what Minnisapa really means. Her brother did a paper on it." Sarah's brother is in the pre-Run-the-World program at Yale.

The guys don't like Sarah's brother, because he's smarter than them. So they start on one of their riffs.

"Minnisapa is Indian for 'Tuesday is Taco-riffic.'"

"Minnisapa is Indian for 'Gee Your Hair Smells Terrific.'"

"Minnisapa is Indian for 'I don't want to have to come up there.'"

"Minnisapa is Indian for 'Burpee's an idiot.'"

"Minnisapa is Indian for 'You want fries with that?'"

"Minnisapa is Indian for 'You're not about to slaughter us and take our land, are you?'"

"Minnisapa is Indian for 'You want to share that remark with the entire class?'"

I just can't stand it anymore. I yell, "Would you guys cut it out. You're being jerks. First of all, there is no language called 'Indian.'"

"Sure, there is," said Smash. "It's like English, but everything ends in 'um'."

I ignore this. "Minnisapa is a Lakota word. And the thing is, Minnisapa doesn't even mean what they told us in school. It doesn't mean 'dark river.' What actually happened was that some stupid white explorer pointed to a map showing the bend in the Mississippi where our town is now and asked the Lakota Chief 'what is this called?' and he answered 'Minnisapa' which doesn't mean 'dark river'; it means 'ink.' The explorer was literally pointing at a blot of ink and the Indian was making a joke at the stupid white guy's expense."

"I guess we had the last laugh," Smash says.

"God will have the last laugh when you burn in hell," I say.

Chimes says, "You're sexy when you're mad" to me. I know he's trying to make things better, but I just stare at the fire all evening.

COMMUNICATIONS

ATTEND A TOWN MEETING WHERE TWO OR THREE POINTS OF VIEW ARE GIVEN.

Quint: Around noon, on a Saturday, coming out from my room and smelling the Pine Sol my mom was using on the kitchen floor, I knew I needed a little fresh air and a lot of not here, so I mumbled back toward the house, "I'm taking a walk" as the door creaked and slammed, but once I started walking I decided I'd shoot some pool at a criminal bar where the bartender never asked for I.D. Of course, there I ran into Burpee, who always looks all scared and birdy, like a sixth grader who walked in the wrong door, and Scott Tulep who looks like he was born in that smudged bar. Then we drove across the river to another bar where we thought, wrongly, that there might be some girls and we drank for most of the afternoon and then we drove around some more and smoked dope and wound up at the house of somebody who lived in some crappy place out in the country and we did something that I think was angel dust but that somebody said was the powder they mix into pigs' feed. This pissed off Tulep and didn't exactly thrill me but we weren't in a position to do anything. These guys were older and nastier than we were. By the time we all wound up at the place where Tulep lives with his dad, things were hissing and flickering and smearing.

If we'd had been with anybody but Tulep, the air would have been a dance partner. The air would have been a comedy.

The furniture looked like it had been beaten-up—tufts sticking out of it, stains like bruises, a nerve-damaged old TV with coat hangers and shit on top of it. We asked Tulep if his old man would mind and he said the son of a bitch hadn't been home in a couple of days. We were sitting there looking at the TV when Tulep got up and said, "It's time for my show." It was such an old-lady thing to say. But I kept my mouth shut. It turns out after some pissed-off fiddling with the antenna and the coat hanger that Tulep's show is a cartoon called Dastardly and Muttley and Their Flying Machines. The premise is that a squadron led by Dick Dastardly has to chase around a carrier pigeon. Dastardly's sidekick is a dog named Muttley who snickers and mutters a lot and who talks that special dog dialect where everything starts with an r. I didn't catch much about the episode, even though no one was saying anything except Tulep who would sometimes cheer them on a little but then he'd be quiet and almost ashamed, the way a dog is when he's eating or shitting.

I laughed when Dick Dastardly took a call on his old lady phone 20,000 feet in the air and Tulep thought I was laughing at him for watching this cartoon and he said, "Shut the fuck up" and I said, "Sorry—everything's funny tonight." After that, Burpee and I simmered in the drugs and pretended we were furniture.

Dick Dastardly is being smacked in the head by this "Pigeon Grabber" thingee when this guy I barely know and already hate shows up at the front door. He's one of those guys who gives himself a nickname and then keeps using it even when nobody picks up on it. He announces, "The Snake has arrived," and we don't pay any attention to him and then he sees what we're watching and he says, "You're watching fucking cartoons?" which is the wrong thing to say and Tulep swivels and says, "This is my house. Shut the fuck up." And then The Snake says, "Don't tell me to shut up," without even thinking and, man, this is one time when you really should be thinking.

Tulep shoots out of his chair and bounces the Snake off a wall and head-butts him and what ensues is less a fight than a detonation that ends up with Tulep choking the Snake and this isn't your playground headlock but a real attempt to snuff the guy out and the Snake knows this—you can see fear igniting in his eyes—and tries to get a knife from his coat, which is a huge mistake because Tulep grabs it and spikes it through the Snake's hand. Snake's scream replaces my mind.

Then I see his hand is ripped and bleeding and stupid as a fish on land. Tulep has straddled Snake and is punching his face again and again. He yells, "Get the fucking knife, Quint." I do. I tighten and toughen. I stand poised; the drugs whoosh from my head. Snake bleeds and cries and squirms. Tulep holds his fist cocked over the Snake's face and says, "Don't you ever come into my house and show me disrespect." He says, "house" like it's a word from the Bible. Finally, the Snake sobs and begs for either Mercy or Mommy.

Tulep relents but keeps the Snake in a headlock and walks him out the door. I ask what I should do with the knife and Tulep takes it in case the Snake comes back with some buddies. While Tulep goes into his dad's room to look for something, I think about mopping up the blood. But I decide I should keep my mouth shut and watch the rest of the show flickering on Tulep's incompetent TV and deal with that rush that feels like electricity and tastes like vomit. Burpee, who had looked so happy to be watching cartoons, now looks lost and like he's about two seconds from crying. I keep staring at the TV while Tulep comes out of his dad's bedroom. We watch Dick Dastardly as he is foiled again in his attempt to catch the pigeon and Muttley snickers something subversive about Rat

Rupid Rick Rastardly and Tulep says, "I love that fucking dog."

As some stupid car commercial comes on, Tulep announces, "Burpee—you didn't do a thing to back me up." In Tulep's head, the fact that I'd pulled the knife out so the Snake couldn't grab it meant I'd been his brother in arms, repelling a common foe. He glares and points at Burpee. "You're not leaving until this place is fucking spotless."

I look at what's left of Burpee tonight and decide it's a not good idea for me to leave, either. As I start pulling an old bottle of Pine Sol and a box of Spic and Span with its torn-open mouth flap out from below the sink, I think for the first time all day of my Mom. She's sitting alone in our living room, trying really hard to concentrate on the TV.

COLLECTIONS

Slow: I make lists. Sometimes with Pooch. Sometimes with a bunch of people sitting at a table on the concourse after school. Sometimes all by myself.

For example, one day in the summer between j-high and senior high, a bunch of us were sitting around playing Monopoly or poker or something at Poochs' house, and we were talking about a kid named Duane Einwald, who had just moved here from some farm town. We decided that he was cool but that "Duane" was a dube name. So we thought about a possible new name, but we kept coming up with strange stuff, and finally Chimes or somebody said, "Wouldn't it be cool if we just gave him a new name every week?" And, for the next three years, we did.

My favorites were:

Duane "Crazy Legs" Einwald.

Duane "Em-Dash" Einwald.

Duane "The Motivator" Einwald.

Duane "The Canadian" Einwald.

Duane "Mature Audiences" Einwald.

Duane "Vocab" Einwald.

Duane "Entropy" Einwald.

Duane "The Widow Maker" Einwald.

Duane "Quadratic" Einwald.

I'm not really sure what he thought of this. He made a face like he was being a good sport but there was a little too much of a wince in there. And, although he spent a lot of time doing art by himself, he would hang around with us some and he bowled with Chimes and Smash. But now I just remember how those names ricocheted around the lunch room or along the lockers. Our high school had the acoustics of a prison. I think most people are flattered when they get a nickname—before he became a complete womanizing, pot-smoking dube, my dad taught me to try to remember to use people's names. But I think Einwald thought we were maybe making fun of him. To be honest, we kind of were.

Pooch and I also once tried to make a list of cool new Merit Badges, which kept being mucked up because we were sitting in the concourse, and people we knew kept stopping by and tossing in their two-cents worth. Pooch had come up with Physics, Calculus, and Board Games as possible Merit Badges and, in the spirit of fun, we suggested a Compare-and-Contrast Merit Badge because that was on every test we took and seemed to be an essential life skill. Somebody passing by said, "Irony. There should be an Irony Merit Badge." While that was a bit much, I did try to look at the good in the suggestion and I came up with the idea of a SitComs Merit Badge. One of the requirements could be, "Discuss with your counselor what makes a good 'wacky neighbor'."

Chimes dropped by and said, "Sitcoms. That would be cool." Chimes was really funny and his A material was wasted on the crowd at the bowling alley where he works.

Then he said, "You should make a list of the Most Asinine Merit Badges. I mean, Pulp and Paper, how lame is that?" I sometimes think that working at the bowling alley has given Chimes a hard edge.

What I couldn't tell Chimes without seeming like a dube is that I love Merit Badges. Every night before I go to bed, after I go through each of my twenty lists, I pull out my sash out and look at each badge and sometimes feel the embroidery like I'm holding a rosary bead. I remember how cool it was to be a kid.

CINEMATOGRAPHY

EXPLAIN AND DEMONSTRATE THE ELEMENTS OF A GOOD MOTION PICTURE. TELL THE STORY. HOW DOES IT READ ON PAPER?

Quint: I remember sitting in this criminal bar on a street ugly with businesses, near a gash of railroad tracks in a part of town where all the houses looked like garages and the sky was the color of a particularly beat-up car. Of course, ninety percent of the guys in there weren't really criminals; they just skipped school and smoked dope and drove with open bottles in the car and planned to go on welfare the minute they graduated, if they did ever graduate. But I was sitting next to Tulep who, I knew, had held up a convenience store just a few days ago and, armed with even more swagger than usual, was proclaiming his philosophy of women.

He leans into me and says, "Quint, when it comes to women, just remember the four *f*s."

"And those would be?" I ask, prompting him like an idiot.

"Find 'em. Feel 'em. Fuck 'em. Forget 'em."

I don't want to tell Tulep that even by my somewhat lax standards, he's an asshole. He owns a gun; he robs stores. So I say, "I tend to have trouble with that last one. The forgetting."

He leans into me. He's got stupid eyes that are just smart enough to know they're stupid and a satanic spike of a chin. Fear swims in my gut, but I reach into the pocket of my navy peacoat and put my hand on my switchblade.

"That's 'cause you're a soft man, Quint. I'm a hard man."

"Yeah, I guess, that's it," I say, and hate myself for agreeing with him. I let go of my blade, though.

Tulep looks into his beer then looks sideways at me and says, "I'm a fucking hard man and don't you ever forget it."

"I won't," I say.

I was tired of these people. I'd signed up for the navy to get out of this life, but wouldn't go to boot camp for four months.

The next day, back at high school, I ran into Sarah Hamilton. I was walking into the library, which wasn't much of a library but which was quiet and carpeted and clean and smelled of new books; it felt like walking into a parenthesis. Sarah was sitting at one of the long tables, with Barb Carimona and some other girls, and they were all trying not to laugh, yet these spurts and sprites and whispers would emerge from their table. They were reading *Without Feathers*, a collection of Woody Allen pieces from *The New Yorker*, but the first thing I noticed after I stopped noticing the girls and their champagne laughter was the book's bright yellow cover, because that cover looked like laughter in a library. I'd noticed Sarah and had a little fantasy about her last fall but didn't really know her. She had moved here before tenth grade when her father arrived to run one of the local companies, and by that time I was already well into delinquency or rebellion or whatever the fuck I was doing so we'd never really gotten to know each other because while she was running the model legislature I was standing in front of Hubie's Neighborhood Foods while it glowed in the night and thinking I was John Coltrane, even though I couldn't be bothered to play saxophone. I smoked like a jazz musician and thought that was a good start. But I'd noticed her that one time before and I'd kept her image with me like a secret cameo although I'd tried not to think of her too much. I knew Barb from way back. I was afraid for her: she exposes too much of her self. I walked up to the girls and asked what they were reading, and Barb told me, but things didn't go much beyond that. Sarah looked up in that shy interested way that some girls have.

Those girls had the faces of girls who'd been good all their lives, and who could breathe a little easier for a few months. You could feel fear of the future and nostalgia for the past tremble inside them, and it seemed particularly concentrated in Sarah. I could tell even then that Sarah's freckles made her ashamed; she considered it a tattoo of wholesomeness. I remember that she had nice eyes but that's just a way of saying, "Nice soul," isn't it?

As I walked away from her, the building changed. I had always hated this place, with its white painted concrete and its linoleum floors and its concourse filled with those stupid pod-shaped plastic chairs and its windowless classrooms, but what had felt like slickness now felt like sweetness. Whoever designed this building wanted to shield us from the swamp and sting of the past, the swamp and sting of ourselves, wanted to make a building as frictionless as dreams. Not the messy dreams you get when you sleep, but aspirations. Inside my head, I soft-shoed like Gene Kelly and, to anyone seeing me, that probably translated into a less-desolate-than-usual slouch.

That night, I bought *Without Feathers* at a bookstore that tried to be a serious bookstore but that had to sell potpourri and gift bears because that is how bookstores survive in towns like Minnisapa. I read the book straight through and then memorized a paragraph. I planned to recite it to Sarah and then ask her out. Selecting what to read had actually proved trickier than I thought. I only knew for sure that she was familiar with the "Selections from the Notebooks" because that's what the girls were reading when I interrupted them. I didn't want to recite the first paragraph because that would look like I hadn't read beyond that. A surprising number of the other entries mentioned killing ("thought: why does man kill?"), sex ("Freud's disciple who discovered sexuality in bacon"), or death ("Once again I tried committing suicide"), none of which were good ice-breakers. I finally decided on the third paragraph:

> **Idea for a story: a man awakens to find his parrot has been made Secretary of Agriculture. He is consumed with jealousy and shoots himself, but unfortunately the gun is the type with a little flag that pops out, with the word "Bang" on it. The flag pokes his eye out, and he lives—a chastened human being who, for the first time, enjoys the simple pleasures of life, like farming or sitting on an air hose.**

That "sitting on an air hose" bit was weird, but it didn't have anything fraught in the first sentence. And it had some natural breaks, so I could stop if things went wrong. The passage was also long enough to impress her.

I'd never asked anybody out before. I wasn't a virgin, but my crowd thought that the whole dating thing was a little too bobby-socks-and-soda-fountain so I'd just wound up with some girl or the other when we were both drunk or stoned and one or two of those pairing-ups had become a boyfriend/girlfriend thing. But I'd never strolled up to a girl sober and said, "Excuse me, Miss, would you like to go out on a date?" It seemed more existential than anything we burnouts had done, a shivering candle of a moment when you said, "Here I am—do you approve?" The plan was to recite the paragraph to her and then she'd be impressed and we would start chatting and, then, casually, I could suggest that we get together for pizza.

It was like a military mission, as I imagined military missions might be from my extensive experience with plastic army men and several viewings of *The Dirty Dozen*: if I blew one thing—if I forgot, if some dork interrupted us—it would all go bad. But it still seemed like the thing to do. I walked up to her between second and third periods. I was both acutely aware and vaguely out of body. Giddiness sparkled in my stomach.

She was half turned toward her locker. "Hey, there," I said, impressing her with my wit.

"Oh, hey there," she said. She was surprised but then remembered me from the library and smiled.

And then I just started reciting, like a kid at the Christmas pageant.

"I just had this"—and then I sped up, in that way you do when you've memorized something, and you want to show off—"idea for a story: A man awakens to find that his parrot has been made Secretary of Agriculture." A couple of kids pushed between us or bumped my back, and I froze, but she started to smile so I just kept on and finished the passage.

"Wow. That's impressive."

"Just a little something I picked up."

"Yeah. Like. Well, very impressive."

We both wanted to flirt but our brains weren't working.

"I wish I could say I had more. But I don't. That's all I memorized."

"And you memorized this for me?"

I didn't think she would be this direct.

"Ahh. Yeah," I babbled. It didn't feel like speech; it felt like verbal drool. I started to panic.

A triangle of guys, reliving their junior high glory days, exchanged shoulder shoves right next to her and one crashed against the lockers. One yelled, "Burpee, you suck!"

This helped: it punctured the moment.

"He's got a point. Burpee does suck," I said. I hated myself for saying that because everybody makes fun of Burpee, but I knew that he would understand because then, I caught my breath and asked, "Would you want to get together for pizza this weekend?"

She paused and her face hardened, with concentration. "I don't know. That sounds fun. I don't know you real well, though." She paused again. "Can I get back to you?" And it struck me how adult that sounded—"Can I get back to you?" Her parents were the kind of people who had day-planners. If most people in Minnisapa had day-planners, they would say, "Go to work. Come home from work. Watch TV."

And so that ended with a whimper but she evidently checked my references with Barb or else she just decided to indulge a self-destructive streak and maybe looked up some program that gave her community service credit for dating me. But, whatever happened, she found me two days later and said, "Yes."

For our first date, we saw Woody Allen's *Annie Hall* on a soft spring night, so everything was perfect—romantic movie and the romantic weather—and yet I was afraid to touch her. It was frightening being with a girl when neither of us was loaded. When we got to Papa Tony's for pizza, I noticed, when I wasn't vibrating with anxiety, that she had these gestures: She had a habit of holding her fingers in front of her—it looked as if she were triangulating a thought.

"I just loved that movie. It was so wonderful. And it was wonderful because it wasn't embarrassed about being intellectual. It didn't just think that thinking was something you did to get a grade or make money. It loved *recreational* thinking."

This charmed me because while people in Minnisapa said

things—"If it ain't one thing, it's the other," "How ya doing," and "Shut up" being local favorites—they never really *formulated* anything. When she talked about something, she would flutter her hand every time she made a new point.

She said, "It could be described as a movie that thought highly of thinking."

She was pleased with this construction, so she jutted out her chin a little and widened her eyes, in a "what do you think of that" way.

When I didn't say anything, right away, because I was trying to formulate something of my own, she said, "That was completely nerdy. My guess is that you don't date many nerds," she said.

"I don't date many girls like you," I said—which, I must admit, was pretty good—and this made her blush. I should have reached across the table and held her hand, but I didn't because I was, what's the word? *chicken.*

She didn't know what to say to that, so I said, "We have to be careful here or they'll take our pizza away. One time a friend of mine—it was Burpee but she didn't need to know that—and I were in here and 'Love Will Keep Us Together' by the Captain and Tennille came on the jukebox. We just *hate* that song so we ran into the bathroom so we wouldn't have to suffer through it and when we came back out our pizza was gone." I noticed then that her laughter and listening were accompanied by a more subtle version of laughter and listening in her eyes.

"You know this place, don't you?" she said.

"What?"

"I mean, I go to school and then I do all sorts of extracurricular things so I'll have a good college application. And then I study at night. And we live in this quasi-suburban lane across Highway 61. The whole point of high school seems to be to keep you from knowing where you live. I mean, I live in Young

Achieverville, USA. I don't want to go to college and then law school and then law practice and never have really known the place where I grew up."

"I know the place where you grew up. It's not that exciting."

"I don't believe you," she said. She suggested a walk.

We walked down some side street with its particular Minnisapa variation on old trees and small houses. If you looked inside you could spy the kind of oil paintings you buy at a drug store and the glow of TVs. I got some confidence back. I started making up a town that was infinitely more interesting than Minnisapa, which isn't that hard to do.

"The man who invented Pop Rocks lives there."

"Mick and Bianca summer there."

"That's where Howard Cosell learned to talk."

"Those people give away diamonds on Halloween."

She laughed. Our hands touched and I almost held hers but pulled back. But she looked at me and said, "what do you feel right now?" and that broke through all the shyness and silliness and we kissed there for a long time, and then she snuggled in close under my arm and stayed there for, like, the next four months. We knew that we just needed that one moment to get through the bullshit and we got it.

That summer Sarah and I saw *Annie Hall* so often it felt like we spent the summer double-dating with Alfie Woodard—the Allen character—and Annie. In my memories, I see them standing there behind the Regal Theater, in the parking lot by Saint Patrick's, which is a little Catholic church, in front of this weird horse and light bulb mural, which was Minnisapa's one attempt at modern art.

Alfie and Annie are standing in that moment that the movie's posters captured: side by side, looking ahead, but edging towards each other, interacting, reacting to something that has been or might be said. She reacts more than he does. She's more subtle, more vulnerable, more decent. They are not American Gothic. There's some hope of communication, some hope of wit, some hope of their faces being turned toward each other, some hope of hope.

I don't know how many times we saw the film. Videos were still a year or two away, and a film like that just wouldn't stay in Minnisapa that long, but we saw it at least two or three times, and when it left Minnisapa we followed it down river to La Crosse, and we had meant to see it in the Twin Cities but had pulled into a motel in a suburb and if there is anything better than sex with a girl you love in a secret motel room when you're eighteen years old, I don't want to know about it because I'll get addicted to it. I still smile every time I see a "sanitized for your protection" wrapper on a plastic drinking glass or smell that chloriney smell or feel those overboiled sheets.

I had a crush on her family, too—don't worry, I once had a crush on a dog. I don't think they were all that crazy about me. But they were unfailingly polite.

She was one of three children in a family where it was expected that you would attend a certain kind of college. When she said, "I want to be the first woman Supreme Court justice," her older brother—who was then a sophomore at Yale—said, without missing a beat, "I'll appoint you." No one else in Minnisapa had those kind of dinner table exchanges.

We would spend hours at her house, which was tucked back in the woods near the country club and which had intercoms between rooms and this huge vaulted wall of glass. We'd read the cartoons and some of the "Talk of the Town" vignettes and comic pieces in *The New Yorker,* which I'd heard about but never read, and the ads—for diamonds, furs, luxury cars, whiskies—would flirt past. The characters in some of the cartoons looked like her family. There was something dimpled and fine to their faces, and a crinkly intelligence in their eyes, that suggested a world different from Minnisapa. They exuded skinny liberal Yankee money and said things like, "They've been perfectly obnoxious ever since they went solar." Or would if they had any peers in Minnisapa to say them to. The Hamiltons were good sports about living in Minnisapa—her dad was the king of the Winter Carnival and wore some big Winter King hat. But they gave the impression of being Foreign Service officers assigned to the colonies.

When I left for the Navy, on one of those late August afternoons that have the dryness and sadness of fall, she walked me down to the bus station. She leaned against me, then held my hand so lightly we barely touched, as if she were rehearsing being apart from me, and then leaned against me again, and there were some kids—I recognized Chimes Sanborn's little brother—starting up a football game in the street and the sight of those kids dodging and yelling made me cry and then we saw Dickie Burpee and his parents on the other side of the street, which was funny because we'd been running into him ever since that time at the lockers, when I first asked her out. But Burpee just waved and didn't say anything because he was also going into the service and he was crying too. And then there was that final embrace where you bury your face down in her neck and you inhale the wonderful scent of her skin and hair as if this is the last moment you will be alive, and you can just feel her shoulders spasm with sobs. And then you are sitting by yourself on a bus and the scenery, which is otherwise pretty nice, just scrapes across your soul.

After about half an hour, for lack of anything better to do, I yell behind me, "How ya doing, Burpee?"

"Totally fucking excellent, Quint." He'd been sniffling, but he had his game face on.

A few weeks later, she left for Columbia. I can't think of two more different places—going from Minnisapa to New York must have been like stepping into an engine, and, like many kids, she wasn't used to not being the smartest kid in class, and she wasn't used to being so far from home. I never knew what it was like to be that on top of anything, to have the cashiers at Bridgeman's recognize your family name when you wrote a check, to have teachers tell you that kids like you were the reason they got into teaching—I was the reason people got *out of* teaching—but I know what it's like to be so connected to a town that you feel that, if you were to spin too fast, the town would spin with you. I know what it's like to know things—some trees, a building with a vent that smells like pizza—so well that they seem to know you.

Like most kids that age, she'd been a tourist visiting despair: sneaking a joint and listening to my blues records. But now despair came looking for her and it wasn't fucking around. She had a breakdown her first term and she took a semester off and lived with her uncle in Evanston, outside of Chicago, and worked in the Newberry Library, a beautiful old research library in the city.

That fall, I was at Great Lakes Naval Base for a month, so we got together. I'd done pretty well in the military: There are times in your life when you just say, "fuck it, tell me what to do," and that was one of them. I did what I was told and, as I got toward the end of my training, I knew what I was doing. But there was something parched and practical about military life, endless days of instruction about the psychology and physiology of air conditioners, nights spent drunk with a bunch of generic "buddies," who managed to make even drinking seem uptight, and crashing on a cot in a Quonset hut. My life became a vast dry colorless loveless thing in which she was the desert flower, so when I had a chance to meet her, we lunged from bar to bar in Chicago, a two-person carnival, and the evening blurred and blared and accelerated and, judging from my missing belt, ended in sex.

The next day, when I met her in this odd long hallway in the library, which was called Rue de Toilette because the johns were at one end, things changed.

We sat at a round metal table, with marble walls on either side. People walked past. Her eyes were shining and wet. Her face was rubbed. This wasn't going to be good.

She was both softer and harder than I've ever seen her. I could see how she would be a businesswoman someday. She was firing me. People kept walking by with their damn lunches and briefcases, but at least they were being loud. At least they were hubbubing it up like good little extras.

"Quint, we had a very special thing. But we can't just rekindle it at will."

"What? Why not?" I, shocked, blurted.

"Well," she said, a little less kind now that I'd raised my voice. "Last night was just kind of desperate and forced. Whatever we had isn't there anymore."

I hadn't noticed anything.

"It's there for me. It's there if we want it to be," I said. I hated women's way of insisting that love was out of the control of either party.

"I was ready for a relationship then, but now I'm not," she said.

"Why not?" I asked. I was just trying to return serve, until I could figure out what to do.

"Quint, you're not like somebody who likes me anymore. You're like somebody who needs a drug."

"So it's not some other guy," I said, which was utterly, smack-yourself-in-the-head stupid. No one in *Annie Hall* ever talked like this.

"No. I just don't want a relationship right now. I don't mean to hurt you."

"Stop saying 'relationship,'" I said. "That's a bullshit word."

"Okay," she said, and then paused, and then started doing that fluttering gesture that always indicated she was thinking about something. "I don't want to hurt you," she started. And that implied that, if she said what was true, she would hurt me. But then a little meanness—no, a little impatience, anger at me for making this hard—sparked across her and she said, "And I don't want to use any, you know, prohibited words."

She continued, "I think that what we had was a . . . romance and that, as a romance, it was very much of its time and place." She ended that sentence with a question mark, an "Am I making sense?" rise to her voice.

And then, after some more silence, she said, "Do you really think you can convince me to love you again?" This time, there was no question mark in her voice. She was just sad and, I think, mad at me for forcing her to be so blunt.

I didn't say anything. I suddenly hated how her family turned everything into discourse.

At the next table, some fuck in a tweed jacket is impressing three co-eds by intoning "naugahyde" with air quotes.

"Now we're just two people with the power to really, really hurt each other," she said. And then, the tears that were shining in her eyes fell.

She started digging in her purse and then held a hankie to her face and sobbed into it twice. The people at the other tables were suddenly being quiet. Assholes.

I said, "Well then, let's not do that. Let's at least not do that." I wanted to end with something noble.

More silence and snuffling. Her hankie was monogrammed.

"I'm gonna go now," I said, because I couldn't stand this anymore and, I'm no dummy, I knew this was over. When I got up, my pants slipped down my waist, showing the top elastic of my underwear. She remembered my belt and started to hand it to me.

I said, and here I swear I really was joking, "All the better to hang myself."

But she said, "Quint, you're scaring me. I know it's just completely paranoid but I'm keeping the belt."

"Fine," I said, and dropped the belt behind me, not even looking back at her, and with that exchange, said good-bye forever.

As I stepped out of the building, shuffling in my loose pants, the world looked uglier than it ever has before or since. I felt a homesickness that could be quenched by no actual place. And I walked out into the syrupy sickening sunlight, towards the suture of the El, which rumbled like a predatory thing, and then, inside the train, I glided past buildings, as ugly as dentures. Why do we see sunlight as anything other than an incidental nuclear cooking?

Why does it gladden us? I straggled off the train at some charmless north side stop and started a drunk that lasted, oh, I don't know how long, because I'm not through drinking yet.

SWIMMING

Slow: It's the summer after high school. We are at an abandoned sand pit called The Quarry, up Highway 61. Here is what is cool about this moment.

1. The sun is high in the sky and burning so brightly I have to squint.

2. From our physics class, I know its rays travel 8.6 minutes to reach my skin, which is exposed but covered with the Savage Tan from Coppertone.

3. The Savage Tan smells like coconuts.

4. The sun is heating the sand to such an extent that it is warm under my 7UP towel and I will have to hot-foot it to scamper into the water.

5. 7UP makes a beach towel, so I don't have to endorse a beer. I drink a beer now and then, but only to not be a self-righteous dube. I don't really like it.

6. The light feeds the cottonwoods that shiver in the breeze and the grapevines that crisscross the sand.

7. The light warms and imperceptibly browns the flesh of the girls near me. Barb Carimona. Sarah Hamilton.

8. Sarah seems to have been a positive influence on Quint King who was level headed in j-high but went dope fiend on us.

9. Barb stands up and lobs a beer to Chimes, who is floating past on his air mattress. It misses by several feet to general merriment.

10. Smash dives in to save the beer. Smash hits the water like a drum stick hitting a cymbal. He comes up without the beer. The girls tease him; their voices are like sunlight on water.

11. Three years on the cross-country team have built up my lungs so I can leap up on some possibly dube impulse and run past everyone and slice into the water, going as deep as I can, viewing the pebbled bottom, the green water, the white bubbles rising to the surface; thinking *this is cool*. I can see the rays of light petering out above me and feel the pressure of the water on me. I flutter around and grope along the sand. My lungs hurt and I'm nostalgic for the air and light. But I clench my lungs and keep looking. Then, just when I'm about to have to come up, my hand touches the smooth heavy glass of the beer and I grab it and surge up toward the sky, holding it aloft. I come up for air a few feet from where Chimes is lolling on the air

mattress. He says, "awesome" and I hand him his beer. Then I bob up and face the shore and there's a rainbow on the surface of my eyes and it illuminates everyone. I'm thinking how cool this is when I suddenly dip down and breathe water and see darkness and feel myself dropping into my grave and with a jolt I pull myself up like I've already done 100 pull ups and my arms are oxygen-starved and dead and I gasp again and my feet still aren't touching bottom so I tread and thrash and tread and thrash but it doesn't seem to be enough and I'm thinking "oh God don't let me die" and the panic is like a movement through water. Smash grabs my shoulder and pulls me up to the air and light and tugs me and I stumble toward the shore, where Quint runs out to help me in and I can hear Chimes is coming up behind us and the girls are standing on the shore white-faced and they wrap me in a towel while I retch and everyone is saying "are you okay? Are you okay?" and Chimes grabs a 7UP from a cooler and hands it to me and says, "a cold one for my man, Slow." I almost cry because everyone is looking at me with gentle faces we never show each other and because Chimes, with the tact of a really good bowling alley manager, says, "a cold one" because he knows that I'm embarrassed that I don't like beer.

BACKPACKING

A list—"Things That Are Very Minnisapa"—compiled by a bunch of people sitting around in the high school concourse and later updated by Slow and taken with him to the engineering program at Iowa State University.

1. That two-story portable cow that's usually outside of Steak Out. Can be rented for parties so that, say, when your kid graduated from Minnisapa State you could honor him by parking a building-sized plastic Holstein in front of his apartment.

2. That signboard where the guy who owned Papa Tony's had spelled out in those black movable letters: "BUY LOCAL PIZZA. NOT CORPORATE PIZZA." ("Pizza places aren't usually that shaming"—somebody around the table.)

3. Those photographs of everybody who was in sports, in some stupid sports-hero pose, that local businesses set in their windows. They were called "Minnihawk Boosters." Note: Pooch and I both have ours.

4. The name "Minnihawks" because it tries to combine "Minnisapa" and "hawks" which were never supposed to be combined. They sound like tiny hawks.

5: Herky Hawk. Mascot for the above-mentioned team, a bulked-up orange-and-black bird. Herky scowls to let you know he means business.

6. The fact that the Minnisapa gay and lesbian organization doesn't include any gays or lesbians—although, in the words of the founder, they "were welcome to join."

7. Broadcasts of fireworks on the radio. Broadcasts of beauty pageants on the radio. This forced the announcers to improvise wildly. "Uh, that's a magenta one. It's kind of blossoming. Oh, that's pretty. This next one's kinda *chartreuse*. Bunch of little stars." Or: "She's dancing to 'Love Theme from Romeo and Juliet.' Very energetic. She's moving her arms a lot. Very graceful. She's clearly put a lot of work into this."

8. The town characters like the old socialist vegetarian who loitered at the co-op all day and wrote these totally incoherent letters to the editor, and the nun who rode a bicycle everywhere and collected cans in bulging garbage bags.

9. The daily "Be Nice To" promotions on the radio station, where the announcers would encourage Minnisapaens to be especially nice to someone that day. Pooch got one when he got some scholarship. Pooch skipped sixth grade, which the

Jaycees think gives him supernatural powers.

10. The fact that the local Go Mart has a donut of the month, and that the donut of the month is named after a Minnisapa "celebrity" and that this is considered a big honor.

SCHOLARSHIP

MAKE A LIST OF EDUCATIONAL PLACES WHERE
YOU LIVE (OTHER THAN SCHOOLS). VISIT ONE.
REPORT ON HOW YOU USED THE PLACE FOR
SELF-EDUCATION.

Quint: Once, when I was in the service, and we were in an Italian port, I stumbled out of the usual sailor neighborhoods, away from the bars sweaty with men and sad with prostitutes, away from the harbor where aborted fetuses floated, and most of all away from my ship, which was like living in an air conditioner the size of five city blocks, in search of something more hopeful. I wound up in some bar where I spied two women/girls who were, I could tell by their preppy air, having their Junior Year Abroad. I was pretty loaded by then, and I'd just gotten paid. A language I didn't know swerved and sparked around me. I walked up to their booth.

"Excuse me," I said. They didn't hear me.

"Excuse me," I said again, this time a little louder.

One of them looked away; the other looked up at me. "Yes?"

"I haven't spoken to an intelligent woman in six months. I will pay you the equivalent of $100 each if you will just tell me the last book you read and what you thought of it."

They looked at each other. I couldn't see their faces clearly. They whispered to each other.

The one with reddish hair looked at me and said, "We don't

want to take money from strange men in bars, but I'll tell you what you want to know. I just read a collection of Franz Kafka short stories. I thought they were very Kafka-esque." She was pleased with the construction, pleased that it had been that easy.

The blonde one—I didn't ask their names—didn't meet my eyes but said, "I just read Dante. I didn't like it. He was a sick man."

They gave me exactly what I asked for; it wasn't anything at all like what I wanted.

I'd leaned forward and put my hands, which concealed the money, on the table. They flinched. I righted myself, leaving the bills behind. "Thank you," I said.

As I was walking away, I wanted to turn back and tell them everything, tell them about a yellow book cover that was like laughter in a library, about *Selections from the Notebooks* and *Annie Hall*, about walking the streets of that Midwestern town with her touching my side and holding my hand, about the way her hands and eyes would move when she formed a thought. But then—and I can't be sure, because bars generate all kinds of birdy, barbed sounds—I was pretty sure they were laughing at me.

Some fat Italian drunk bumped into me as I was walking out of the bar, so I grabbed him and rammed him into a brick wall until he started to scream and bleed. He wasn't drunk, but the bartender's retarded brother.

CANOEING

Chimes: We missed the concourse like it was a limb, but none of us wanted to be one of those people who kept going back to high school. So I brightened when Smash and I were sitting at the bowling alley and Slow and Pooch and then, five minutes later, Barb all came through the door. It was spring break of their first year in college.

People started riffing, just like old times. Of course, Slow sounded like everybody's dad, Smash blurted stuff, Pooch worked out complicated shit in his head, and Barb sometimes seemed baffled, like a smart person who's just woken up. But it felt like, together, we were one incredibly smart person.

Slow declared, "We've decided that this is the new concourse."

"Hey Barbie, look out for flying orange halves."

She looked at Smash, disgusted, yet complimented. "Where's that scary man who owns this place . . . Jimbo?"

"Jimbo's golfing," I said.

Pooch said, "Man, I'd love to see that. He might actually be able to alter the rotation of the earth by smacking it with a golf club."

There was a silence. I was a little nervous, because this was different from making fun of Jimbo in the concourse. He was my boss here.

But they couldn't resist, and I couldn't bring myself to tell them to stop.

Slow said, "Jimbo might have the worst customer service skills of anyone who actually has a job."

Smash went into an immediate imitation of my boss: "You didn't pay for nice."

Pooch yelled, "You think 'pleasant' grows in trees."

Barb corrected him: "On trees."

Smash slammed his fist at Barb, and yelled: "Never correct me, woman! I'll kill you!"

Barb jumped a little, then said, "He is *really* grumpy."

Slow said, "There are like three guys who are grumpier than he is. And they're behind the Iron Curtain."

Pooch: "Jimbo Lane, thrown out of Romania for being . . .

Barb: ". . . surly . . ."

Pooch: " . . . started a new life in Minnisapa, Minnesota."

At that point, the phone rang. It was someone at the hospital, saying that Jimbo had a heart attack. In the ambulance, he'd dictated a to-do list for me. The big one was take over the bowling alley. Jimbo wouldn't work another day.

Sometime the next week, one of the kids who now worked for me said, "I know I shouldn't say this, but it's so much better around here now that you're in charge. I don't get sick to my stomach coming to work."

"Nicest thing anyone's ever said to me."

Something else happened that day, but for obvious reasons I didn't notice it. Pooch would throw Christmas bashes; people might show up one by one at the alley; Smash would leave town for months and then careen back; the odd bachelor party would get the guys together—Smash actually proposed to a stripper at one while Slow winced with embarrassment—but it would be years before we would all be together like this again.

BIRD STUDY

FIND THE CHRISTMAS BIRD COUNT NEAREST YOUR HOME AND OBTAIN THE RESULTS OF A RECENT COUNT . . . IF THE NUMBER OF BIRDS . . . IS DECREASING, EXPLAIN WHY, AND WHAT, IF ANYTHING, COULD BE DONE TO REVERSE THEIR DECLINE.

Barb: I'm in a movie theater in Minnisapa, one of the old, pretty ones from before the multiplex. "Hey, Berf." "Hey, Berf." "Hey, Berf." "Hey, Berf." "Hey, Berf." They—the two guys I'm with, the two guys who are joining us—are yelling across the theater. They all share the nickname "Berf," which they have taken from an old *Dick Van Dyke Show* episode. I think it's the name he called his brother. People look up, annoyed. Some kid—not getting the joke—says, "Who's Berf?" Smash, who got his name for his aggressive ping-pong playing, and who, of all of these guys, is the one I'm most interested in, says, "Her boyfriend." I'm sixteen and clueless and without a boyfriend, so I blush and turn my head away in the darkness so that no one can see my neon emotions. All these years later, I blush again.

I am in New York, tired of stepping out of the office after work and discovering that the snowflakes that floated so serenely past the firm's eleventh-floor windows have been turned to crap by the city—by the taxicabs stampeding everywhere, by the men who hawk food, by the steaming waterpipes, and by the crush of foot traffic. I am tired of the pushing of strangers and tired of the sewer and garbage smell and tired of the filth and honking and tired of being twenty-two and never having any money and living in some crap place in Jersey. I am tired of the whole celebration of asshole-dom which is New York. I want to go to a place where the snow stays white and beautiful, where it is not pulverized the second it hits the ground, and where people at least make an effort to be kind. I want to go home.

I am on a plane from New York to Minneapolis. When we have been aloft for some time, I look out the plane window, and see beautiful grids of lights. As we approach the Midwest, the clusters of lights become smaller; the darkness that surrounds them becomes larger. These clusters are towns—not the vague tri-state areas of the east, not the usual stupid subdivisions and suburbs—but towns. The entire country is a single Christmas decoration. I feel like an angel stumbling across the horizon toward a bright light; I feel that all those people—including me, most of the time—who say that traveling is not the point of Christmas are dead wrong. Traveling is exactly the point of Christmas. The wise men were probably exhausted; half-lost; bitching at each other about when they should stop, where they should go; they were probably totally fed-up; those ancient priests were pulled by a star that felt like the purest love they had ever known. And so, totally pissed off, barely talking to each other, slapping their stupid camels, they trudged on.

Arriving in Minnesota is like landing in a Sears catalog. I'm greeted by my parents, who are studies in polyester. My mother wears powder-blue pants; my father, navy blue. Down parkas fatten both of them.

"Hello, dear. It's so nice to see you," my mother says, as she hugs me and I—awkward, burdened by bags, slightly staggered by the background noise and peripheral dramas of the airport—hug her back, though less vigorously than she hugs me. Of the three kids, I'm the only one who has returned for Christmas. My brother is in the service in Germany; my sister has a newborn in California.

My father asks, "Can I take your bags, or are you a woman's libber?" Believe it or not, my father is a professor. He wrote a pamphlet, aimed at bright eighth-graders, called "The Geology of the Minnisapa Area." It's in my purse.

Waking after the ride home (I slept with my face smushed into the upholstery of the back seat, breathing in its scent), I stumble out the car door. Despite the strips of exposed silver insulation, the garage is chilly. A rake and some garden implements hang on the wall along with the tandem bike my parents bought for themselves the summer after I left home, their first alone in more than twenty years. I had thought that my departure would bum them out, but the bike suggests that it liberated them. Oh, well.

After the briskness of New York, I'm amazed at how suddenly inefficient I am, how—as I loiter in my nightgown, on their couch—hours slip by with nothing in them but commercials and cups of coffee. How much staring, how much daydreaming, how much poking around in magazines, how much slackness that doesn't sweeten into sleep, how much walking to and fro and forgetting what I'm looking for, how many odd little forgotten chunks of time. I dismiss the *Minnisapa Daily News* to the coffee table. It's not innocent and cute anymore. Some stupid corporation bought it and turned it into a tabloid because they sit in board rooms and talk about how stupid Joe Sixpack is and congratulate themselves on their realism. There's a big picture of a car wreck on the front page. Car wrecks sell papers, but they aren't what makes Minnisapa special. The former owner of the paper was an ornery old reactionary but he knew what made Minnisapa special.

I lean back in the couch and press the remote, which incites the television. "Family Feud," with the faux sampler logo. I hate Richard Dawson. I turn down the volume, which my parents had cranked. They have aged. The TV is too loud, the place is too hot.

"I can't believe they've got pro wrestlers on Family Feud," I say. "Who thought of this?"

My mother's voice comes from the kitchen. "No one told you to watch it, dear."

"I'm not watching it. It's just on, and I don't know why we excuse every piece of crap in this country by saying, 'You don't have to watch it.'"

Having finally showered and dressed, I step into the kitchen and experience that wonderful switching of senses you get with baking; it smells warm and feels sugary, spicy. The oven ticks.

My mother flattens cookie dough with a rolling pin. There is something gentle about the way she rolls it, a wistful little easing up at the end of the roll. "I'm sorry I was so snappy," she says.

"That's okay," I say.

"We don't have you for that long. There's no reason for bickering," she says.

"Is there ever?" I ask, still a little cranky.

"It's a part of life. People get into moods." She presses a tin cutter into the dough, creating plump, scallop-edged cookie men.

I open the white cookie jar decorated with blue flowers and the cloudy Tupperware bins and discover star-shaped cookies dyed red and green, ice-box cookies, sugar cookies in the shapes of Christmas trees and candy canes, divinity, anise, banana cookies, pocket cookies filled with raisins and dates. "You accept too much, Mom."

She tugs the little men from the dough. They are fragile and sagging, so she places them across her fingers and guides them onto the cookie sheets, like a medic lowering a patient onto a stretcher. She applies white frosting to cookies that have been cooling and arranges red candies for their mouths and silver ones for their eyes.

"They don't have noses," I point out.

"They don't have handkerchiefs, either," she says. "They'll just have to do without."

I'm standing too close to her—there's this difficult weather swirling between us—so I sit down at the table.

She sets another batch of dough on the cutting board. "It scares me when you talk as if you'll accept nothing but a perfect world. I'm afraid too much is going to pass you by."

"High standards mean that less passes you by," I say, suddenly all haughty.

"No. It should work that way, but it doesn't. You have to forgive the world to enjoy the world."

"Whatever," I say, although I'm more baffled than anything.

She creates six more little men.

Early the next afternoon, I drive to the Happy Chef for breakfast.

The houses have shrunk and seem weirdly sheepish. The houses don't want to be called on. It hasn't snowed in a while, so the snow is dirty, and the sky is the color of clinical depression.

On the radio, the Minnisapa station announces that a dog—a collie named Roger—has been lost and provides a description and a phone number. A tear moistens my cheek.

The restaurant is almost empty. I sit at a booth and stare out the window at the Happy Chef sign—a chubby, rosy chef in a doughy hat—in the parking lot. The sign used to have a button on it and, when you pressed it, this surprisingly hostile recorded message would play. "If you park here, the Happy Chef will crush you with his spoon." Really, that's what he said.

I get some totally malignant looks from two people at the first booth—a massively fat woman and her preposterously skinny man. He is so skinny that his beard seems super prominent, like the salt jutting from a pretzel. She is so fat that it looks as if unbaked dough were applied directly to her, without being digested first. They both look at me with the anger they must feel at God.

The waitress, an older woman with frosted hair and pale glossy lipstick, looks out at the sky as if divining something.

"They say maybe a little snow," she says. Her voice is kind and thin, still very Minnisapa, but not what I expected. "I love a white Christmas," she says, acknowledging, perhaps without knowing that she is doing so, that what we have now—this tired old snow—isn't really white.

"Yes, I'd like that too," I say in my best leaders-of-tomorrow voice.

"You going to school?" the waitress asks.

"No, I graduated from the U a little while ago. I live in New York now."

"Oh, that place would scare me. All those muggers. My granddaughter's about your age. She ran into a little trouble in high school, got pregnant, married some jerk, but she's going to the vo-tech now and taking the cosmetology, and she just loves it."

"Good for her," I say. "Sometimes I think you appreciate school more after you've been in the world some." It's something I've heard my father say.

"It looks like you had your hair done. That's very modern." She doesn't put any snotty spin on "modern"; she likes it. I have cut my hair short and spiked it a little with mousse. It is fashionable in New York. It isn't fashionable here; nothing is fashionable here.

The waitress touches my hair, gently, like it's good luck, and she makes me feel like a charmed being. I blush a little, but it's okay.

I sip my coffee, which in Minnisapa is just discolored hot water, and stare out the window while I eat. In the middle distance, there's an intersection where the street I grew up on merges onto new Highway 61 and a bunch of other roads. A strip mall, a motel, and a pizza place occupy the other side of the intersection. Behind that are hills I climbed as a girl. The hills are brown and bare now, whiskery with trees, but in summer they are beautiful and almost exuberant. The hills are sandstone and limestone, deposited by prehistoric lakes, cut by the Mississippi. That is what the pamphlet my father wrote told me.

I finish my massive order of waffles, tug some napkins from the chrome holder, and leave a large tip. The waitress has been nice, and I decide that I am all for niceness. I mean real niceness, not the kind of niceness most people mean, which is just the way middle-class people congratulate themselves for not hitting each other. Real niceness makes you feel better. It moves something in your heart and warms you, and it is really very rare.

When I am walking past the couple in the booth, the woman snorts at me: "Nice hair." I turn to—what? Not exactly confront her—but she is looking down, as if she never said anything, as if I would be a very mean person to suggest that she did.

In the car, I turn on the radio, and a Minnisapa show called *Party Line*, this weird classified advertising for the radio, comes on. The first caller I hear says, "How much for that case of cream corn then?"

Later in the afternoon, it begins to snow. As I gaze out my parents' living room window—and it really is a gaze; the snow deepens my stare into contemplation—the sky is this gorgeous purple. Large, slow-falling flakes. Sometimes you watch snow falling, and it looks like an act of love. It is that gentle; it is that generous. When I leave to walk three blocks to a party that Pooch Labrador throws every Christmas, the snow sparkles and froths. The way light moves through that snow, and the way the snow moves through the air—perfectly agile, ready to be airborne again even after it has fallen—it's as if the landscape itself understands joy. I wish I could stay in it. I consider walking around town, building snowmen, playing like a kid, but I need to—as a proto-adult—attend this party.

Pooch's parents' kitchen seems faintly sabotaged. It's probably something simple—new photos in different frames, an avocado refrigerator replaced with a white one. But it feels spookier than that.

It soon becomes apparent that houses change, but people

stay pretty much the same. Three guys from my high school gang are sitting in the kitchen. The women they brought have been deposited like housewarming gifts in the living room, far enough away that they don't have to be introduced. The guys always outnumbered the girls, and it seems that I am the only girl from the old crowd, which makes me feel particularly unprotected.

"Barb."

"Pooch."

"Barb."

"Chimes."

"Barb."

"Slow."

"Beer?"

"Yes."

Chimes gets me a beer and says, "So our little Barbie is all grown up and spiking her hair."

Of course, my hair is the first thing he notices.

"Fuck you," I say. This isn't a crowd that swears much.

Smash enters from the basement rec room and asks, "What did I miss?"

"Barb told Chimes to fuck off," Pooch reports. "That's about it."

"Cool. Nice 'do, Barbie. Very Pat Benatar."

"Fuck you, too."

Without saying anything, Chimes and Smash shake hands, as if they had just formed a fraternity based solely on the fact that I had rebuked both of them. I am tired of being the butt of jokes because I do things and say things. These guys just wait for other people to do things and say things so that they can make snide little comments on them.

Later, for lack of anything better to do, I descend to the basement for ping pong, which strikes me as incredibly weenie, but at least it's a chance to do something, to move. Of course, we play ping pong surrounded by the stacks of *National Geographics* that everyone in Minnisapa has in their basement. All our parents must have subscribed at the same time; it's like they must have felt that they should signal to us—secretly, without saying anything—that the world is a larger place than Minnisapa. I, however, appear to be the only one who got the hint. How I wish I were in New York and very drunk and dancing to very loud music. In New York, I have learned that dancing doesn't have to be an embarrassed shuffle. It can be a scream. It can be just what your soul needs. But not in this house, and not in this town.

Pooch and I have been playing for some time. I am losing but not by much.

Slow is watching and announcing. "Barb's behind but she has demonstrated her ability to rally in the past." Slow is trying to make me feel good. He is weirdly responsible about that kind of thing, a miniature dad. But tonight it just feels kind of patronizing. And also, excuse me, it's a ping-pong game.

Pooch taps his shot long and to one corner. I return it. He approaches and spins it to the part of the table away from me. I spin and smack it with both hands and my entire body like I'm driving a backhand in tennis. It ricochets off the concrete-block walls in a way that makes everyone flinch. The ball bounces and romps and won't sit still. It's like someone has let a bird loose in the basement and they don't know what it's gonna do.

"Jeez, Barb. Settle down," Slow says in his patriarchal way, which he adopts despite the fact that he's like four days older than me.

"Oops. I'm such a girl," I say. There are three more serves. I hit each one as hard as I can at a different wall and start to laugh that laughter that you can't quite control but that feels super delicious as it moves through you. This is totally worth it. I shake so hard I drop my ping-pong paddle and then I almost sob.

Pooch and Slow are trying to find the ping pong ball under a couch and wondering why I'm such a psycho. I go upstairs for another beer.

I am talking to someone's fiancée, a small woman with a prim little helmet of hair. I believe she teaches preschool, not because of anything she says, but because she has a tone in her voice that implies we might all swallow our Cracker-Jack prizes if she doesn't watch out for us. She asks me if there is anyone *special* in my life. I hate her for implying that I need someone to make my life not merely special, but acceptable, but I am not quite drunk enough to confront her, although I'm getting there. As I'm talking to her—she's the kind of tight ass who makes you feel drunk even when you're sober—she keeps looming—I want to scream, "STOP LOOMING!" Other things I shouldn't say form and hover in my mind. I overhear Slow and Pooch, who must have rescued the ping-pong ball, doing a routine they often did—talking in farmer voices—only now it is about me. "Oh, that Barbie. Her dad teaches the geology there. Yeah, the guy knows more about a rock than anybody. Well, that Barbie, she went and got her hair moussed, just like those communists."

"Those communists with their moussed hair."

"Don't get me started on those Trotskyites and their mousse."

"But what exactly is so funny?" I say louder than I meant and people turn around. "Come on, answer me, dammit." I knock into the preschool teacher, who says, "Excuse me?"

I ignore her; I ignore them because I've changed my mind—I

have a plan, a plan which involves me yelling until I get everyone's attention: "HEY! NO. HEY! NO. HEY! NO. NO. LISTEN TO ME! WE NEED TO PLAY TWISTER!"

I think that I will knock away their stupid small-town defenses. I wobble, my thoughts lurch. I am the only woman to participate, so Chimes and Pooch and Smash and I lunge and contort until we, I believe, knock Pooch off, because Chimes and Smash and I keep bumping shoulders and crossing limbs and pushing torsos into each other, and then I think Chimes falls down because, as we dive for the next colored dot, Smash winds up straddling me and says, "Bummer about the clothes," and I say "What's wrong with your clothes?" and then I get that he means that, given the position we're in, it's unfortunate we are wearing clothes at all. Then there's this snickering, which might come from the women on the periphery— who knows, when your face is mashed into a plastic tarp, and you're this loaded?—and the snickering is followed by a sort of clucking as I, having twisted my butt into the air, support myself on my trembling aching wrists (I can see a pink line forming where they hinge) and I stare at green polka dots and smell the beer on Smash's breath and the nostalgic smell of the plastic Twister tarp and then I hear one more cluck from somewhere on the periphery, from some Future Housewife of America, and I just snap. I stand up and scream, "Go to hell," and then I bump past some shocked people, and something swims and tickles in my stomach, and I vomit as I reach the kitchen, the contents of my stomach pushing and splattering in front of me—it's horrible, I want to stop and cry and apologize for everything, I can see everything I ate at Happy Chef on Pooch's parents' kitchen counter—but I can't bear to stop, so I grab my coat and stumble out into the cold. I carry my unspoken apologies with me like a thief.

The air is cold and clean and clears my head when I breathe it in, but I still stumble. I sense some of the guys following me for a while. Then I confront a snowman and decapitate it and fall down next to the severed snowman head. I stuff my mouth with snow to get rid of the taste of vomit. Then, the stars surprise me.

The sky starts to spin. I close my eyes and press my face in the snow to keep myself from vomiting again. I hear the guys yelling to each other; they have fanned out, like they did when we all played ditch as kids and searched the darkness for each other, when we were twelve and out past dark for the first time and the prospect of losing and finding each other made me afraid and happy at the same time, and then I feel someone—I think Pooch—tugging at me and calling to the other guys and then I am walked home, Pooch and Slow on either side of me, their arms around me, keeping me from falling or veering, listening to me sob and mutter, "What's wrong with me? What's wrong with me? What's wrong with me?"

High school. The chaos of fifteen hundred lockers slamming. Those brisk moments between classes. A banner hanging from a wall says, "Positive Mental Attitude."

"Duane 'The Motivator' Einwald!" Chimes is calling to poor Duane, whose nickname changed constantly   from "Crazy Legs" to "The Canadian" to "Vocab"—and I never figured out why it changed.

"Chimes, is there some, like, secret principle to this?"

"There is, Barb. But we all agreed that we can't tell you what it is."

WOOD CARVING

COMPLETE A SIMPLE LOW RELIEF PROJECT.

Chimes: Smash Sarnia's an orphan—his Aunt raised him—and my theory is that it's always given him a wild edge, so that he acts the way normal people would if they suddenly woke up on Mars. You'd kind of go ape shit and start running around and screaming because there weren't any fucking people on this planet and you were freezing your nuts off and you had no idea how you got here.

Most every Christmas, he'll call me from some bauxite mine in Utah or convenience store in El Salvador and give me his "You and Pooch are the only real friends I've ever had and that's not just the booze talking" speech. But this year he showed up, after driving this crappy Canadian Pinto for about two days straight through a blizzard in Quebec, where he was—get this—the Social Director at a Nursing Home. I have no idea how in the hell he got a work permit or whatever, and I didn't ask. Asking questions like that is like asking where Wile E. Coyote got the dynamite. In fact, Pooch, who was back early to get some scholarship, and I had a little talk about that at the bowling alley I manage. I think he said something like, "Chimes, I think Smash is just lucky to be allowed in his own country."

Smash walks in the door of the alley and yells, "Chimes! How the hell are you!" which startles the natives who are, believe me, easily startled. He's clearly a man who's been driving for about thirty years straight. His clothes look like shit and he's tired but plugged into something. Nothing chemical; other than booze, chemicals are redundant with Smash.

"Check this out! I can't unclench my fucking hands." He's amazed, like we were still kids poking around by the Mississippi and he'd found an arrowhead. He makes this claw motion to show off his hands and then shimmies to get his back straightened.

I was so glad to see him, the first ten beers were on me.

He crashed on the floor of my apartment that night and then we went to Happy Chef for breakfast that next afternoon, so hungover we'd actually moved down the evolutionary scale a couple of notches, and we swore we saw Barb Carimona pulling out in her dad's car as we were pulling in, which was another great sign. I think we even high fived when we saw her. You can't help but love Barb; she's never quite learned that everything isn't supposed to be on the surface and unlike some of our friends, she thought that at least one point of life was to have the occasional smidgen of fun.

The summer after high school, before Smash left for wherever the hell it was he left for, Barb and he and I hung out at the Quarry, an old sand mine which had filled with incredibly pure water and was surrounded by grapevines and birches and these trees whose leaves made this cool shimmering noise in the breeze. We'd show up with sixteen-ounce Budweisers and buckets of Kentucky Fried Chicken and splash on this coconut-scented suntan oil that still smells like good times to me. Other people would appear, like on sitcoms: Quint King and Sarah Hamilton, who had become an unlikely item, the rebel and the class president, and, of course, Pooch was a fixture. Einwald, who I think we were calling "Bubbles," made a cameo or two. Slow would stop by. Slow, who was always intense, was especially intense that summer. He was the only eighteen-year-old male in the world who didn't understand the concept of Getting Laid, and spent all his time scanning the horizon for a nice girl who would make a suitable life-mate. Once he dove underwater to save a beer for me—yes, a beer—and nearly drowned himself. Smash and I started calling him Slow Slocum, underwater bartender, but he didn't think it was funny. Yeah, he's nuts, but Slow and that whole crew and I have been friends since forever. For one summer, our lives were a beach movie. How often in life can you say, "Everybody I give a shit about is within ten feet of me?" I think we knew that things would never be this cool again. I hadn't seen Barb in two years and Smash hadn't seen her in four.

The party that night wasn't as much fun as we'd thought it would be. But, then, are they ever? Barb had gotten all bitchy on us. We were kind of assholes, but then we're always kind of assholes—although, I must say, charming ones—so that couldn't be it. Then, after a promising game of drunk Twister, she flat out, literally ran away from us. She threw-up halfway out the door, which ruined the Contessa effect, not to mention Pooch's parent's toaster. We evidently weren't as cool as her New York friends, which pissed us off on the surface and which we couldn't admit really broke our hearts. And the rest of those guys suddenly just seemed boring. I think Slow was elaborating on his theory that you shouldn't screw your wife until you could afford a house, that bringing children into the world of rental property was wildly irresponsible. Although I must say that those guys found our poor drunk Barbie, stumbling around out there, with snow falling on her, and made sure she got home safe and sound.

We half-heartedly looked for her but then split and went to a bar across the river—they're open later in Wisconsin, which is just brilliant. Let's encourage drunk driving. We arrived at this juke joint, sitting at a wobbly little table with somebody else's beer-soaked napkin on it. Everybody was wearing green-and-orange parkas that made them seem even fatter and uglier than they already were. While we were scanning the place for unattached women and not finding any, some guy who recognized me from the bowling alley, walked up to me and said, "Pretty loaded." It wasn't clear if he meant that he was pretty loaded, or that I was, or that pretty loaded was just a worthy goal, and he teetered, so I said, "Yeah, been partying pretty hard," which is what you have to say to get rid of these clowns, and he raised his beer to me and walked away.

Somebody bumped our table and we dove for our beers, and that summed up the pointlessness of this little sojourn.

"Let's get out of here before I punch one of these idiots," Smash said, and we left, somehow navigating several miles of snow-slicked road, which was like driving on a ski run, and then over the Mississippi bridge and getting past the cops without killing ourselves.

Later, we just sat in my apartment, drinking, Smash on my crappy sofa, me against the wall. By about three thirty in the morning, things were getting pretty blurry; I'm nobody's idea of a lightweight, but I'm not used to that kind of pace. Smash was. I felt like I was being dragged behind a car.

Smash was talking about who you can trust.

"You go through this fucking world, and there are so many

people you just can't trust."

"Yeah," I said, because that's what you say at times like that. I have no idea whether I actually agreed with him.

"But then there are the guys you can trust."

I think I agreed with that, too. I wanted to get to sleep.

"What's the ratio of people you can trust to people you can't," he said. He would not shut up. "It sucks. The thing's backwards. There should be like a million guys like you and Pooch and then a couple of assholes, to keep people honest. God's an idiot." Smash, the theologian.

He shut up for a while, then said. "And what's Barb's problem?"

"Who knows?" I said. "It's one thing to tell guys that they're losers. But to make a special trip from New York just to tell guys that they're losers . . . Man, that's just mean."

"That was so incredibly cool when we saw her in the Happy Chef parking lot," Smash said. "I was actually looking forward to Pooch's stupid party." Smash was a little more in touch with his feelings than guys in Minnisapa are supposed to be. There are rules to living here, and Smash doesn't give a shit about them and Barb never seems to have learned them, but I know what they are. You can't run a bowling alley in this town if you're always saying things that nobody in this town ever says. There are two acceptable things to say about women you like: "It was good to see her." Or: "I wouldn't mind nailing her." You might say, "I think I like her." The "I think" is crucial. You have to make it clear that you don't spend too much time hanging around your own emotions, so your intelligence about them might be unreliable.

"Man, it really was great to see her," Smash said again. "My whole body smiled."

All of this somehow led to the usual talk about how your friends don't bullshit you the way women do. That led to the subject of blood brothers, which Smash wanted to formalize. We did this blood brothers thing in junior high once with Pooch. Found some stick pins in Smash's aunt's medicine cabinet and pricked ourselves and rubbed the blood together. It was during our mix-hairspray-and-Hai-Karate-and-light-them-on-fire phase. Doing things that lame is the point of being that drunk, so I said, "Okay." Smash had driven for days to get to Minnisapa, and this was as close at he was going to get to a highlight reel.

That's when he reached into his duffel bag and grabbed this six-inch bowie knife.

Oh, fuck, I thought.

"I'll go first," he said.

"Smash," I said, "This isn't a good idea. Trust me. You're my buddy. Always have been. Always will be."

But he didn't hear me and started chopping at his thumb and wrist.

I froze. He started bleeding; at first, it looked like there was Chinese writing on his thumb and the top of his hand, but then it just got messy, and I said, "Okay, give it to me."

"No, we gotta make sure," he said and kept hacking.

He passed out then, dropping the knife away from him. I found some toilet paper and wrapped up his hand, which kept twitching, but the toilet paper turned red; I think I pissed him off; he gurgled something at me; I sat and stared and hoped like hell the bleeding would stop and kept putting more and more toilet paper on it and squeezing his damn hand until it finally stopped. It felt like an hour.

When I woke up the next afternoon, Smash was gone but he had left a note on a chunk of old pizza box, saying, "Great to see you, dude. That was intense. Gotta run so I don't lose the stupid job. I like those old Canadian geezers. Merry Christmas. Smash." There was blood on my carpet and couch. I didn't do much that day, all three hours of it, just drank a lot of coffee and took about eight showers and drank a gallon of chocolate milk. Then I showered one more time and got ready to go over to my parents' for Christmas Eve.

And oh yeah, this: I found a serrated kitchen knife and gritted my teeth and sawed my thumb until lines of blood formed. I sawed deep enough that the next time Smash saw me, even if it was fifty years from now, even if I was dead, he could look at my hand and tell that, somewhere on this frozen planet, he'd had a brother.

ENGINEERING

STUDY THE ENGINEER'S CODE OF ETHICS. EXPLAIN HOW IT IS LIKE THE SCOUT OATH AND SCOUT LAW.

Slow: I proposed to Kelly a few days after the party where Barb Carimona threw up on Pooch's parents' toaster. Kelly took a breath like you do before diving into cold water, smiled, and said, "Yes." A few days after that, we were at Bridgeman's. The waitress was a high school girl who was so cheery she might as well have been carbonated; the décor was so white it made you want to brush your teeth; and there was a young family with two cute little girls across from us who looked like a postcard from our future. And then, like a dube, I said, "You should attend confession, to start the marriage pure."

She said, "What?" in the way that she talks when she's impatient with me. Her face hardened a little. She's a medical student, which gives her a no-nonsense approach to life.

I said, "What I meant is that we should both go to confession. I hadn't meant that I was pure and you weren't."

But she looked at me as if this irritated her more.

"I've always liked the fact that you're really principled, but sometimes . . ." she said. She sighed.

"You don't think we should go to confession before we get married?" I asked.

She softened her expression and raised her fingers to touch her hair. But she'd cut it recently, because she didn't want it hanging in cadavers when she went back to med school. So she played with the memory of her hair. She said, "I guess. But, I don't know . . ."

"What's not to know?" I said. "You either believe in the sacraments or you don't. You either think premarital sex is a sin or you don't." I knew I was right, but I also knew I should have shut up.

"Can we just not talk about this right now?" she said.

We'd ordered our food, so we couldn't leave. We'd both ordered huge phosphates to go with our sandwiches. When the waitress delivered them, they were about the size of Christmas trees. Mine was green; hers, cherry red. The waitress said, "Now can I get you guys anything else?" and smiled.

Kelly had swiveled her head away from the waitress and was staring at the space between the booths. I was the one who'd ruined the evening, so it was my job to make it clear to the waitress that we didn't need anything else.

"No, we need to catch a movie, so if we could have the check, that would be great." I had told a lie. There was no movie.

Our faces were the only thing in the place that weren't happy. Kelly looked down and away in one direction and I looked down and away in another direction. We didn't talk much. It was one of those rare times when you're nervous *after* you do something. One of the little girls started screaming and that was a relief.

Still, I was aware of every crunch of toast and lettuce and chicken in my mouth. I slurped my phosphate too hard, and it gurgled.

"Sorry," I said.

"For what," she asked. Her voice was still hard.

"For gurgling like I was in j-high."

"Don't worry about it."

I was hoping she'd soften up but she didn't. When the waitress brought back the check, she gave me this look like whatever had happened between Kelly and I might be her fault, for being a bad waitress. She was a good kid, the kind of girl who views smiling as a distinct activity, a gift that she consciously shares with the world. I smiled at her enough to make it clear that it wasn't her fault, but not so much that it looked like I was flirting, and I left a big tip.

As we were putting our coats on, I said, "You know I didn't mean that I thought I was pure and you weren't."

"Didn't we agree not to talk about this?" Kelly said without quite bothering to turn around all the way. It was January and we both were really aware of how big our parkas were. We were dressed like snowmen. She turned to walk in front of me, so I almost had to jog to catch up.

The next thing I knew she was giving me my ring back. It was one of those talks with girls that begins with them saying, "I really love you," and then calling you by name. You would think that the best conversations would start, "I really love you, fill-in-the-blank," but when girls think about a conversation like that, they think like engineers. They frontload the conversation with a really cool thing to hear so that when they tell you that they've concluded that you're really a dube, it balances out. But the problem is that those conversations are more like calculus than like algebra; each variable changes the other variables. In other words, guys know what's coming, so, when they hear, "I really love you," in that tone of voice, they change its value to a negative. Still, I think she was trying to be decent about it, and I try to remind myself of that.

She told me the usual break-up stuff—*might be the biggest*

mistake of her life, I was great, etc. She even said she thought it was cute that I was concerned about the fact that we'd had sex before marriage, which struck me as patronizing. But then she said that the problem was the whole going-to-confession-because-she-wasn't-pure thing, which I tried to explain again. But she said that there really was more to it, that being married to me would be too much like being in a cult, and that even though saying that was unfair, it was the best she could do. I kept trying to argue with her, but then I thought, you don't really want someone to marry you because they lost a debate. We ended two years with one of those lame, awful break-up hugs.

And then, like a week after Kelly called it off, I got a call from the top engineer of the company I'd gotten an offer from, a place that made home appliances. I was totally psyched about this job, where I imagined myself undoing the design missteps of the Seventies, and designing the Home of the Future, stuff with unexpected push-button capabilities and teardrop-shaped touch screens and colors from the 50s and grilles like smiles and sans-serif Swiss fonts that make you feel like you've been scrubbed clean. (Europeans are dube but they're great at typography.) I would sometimes study one of the lists in my drawer: my ten favorite appliances. Attached to the list was an old ad for my favorite, the Camfield toaster. It was described as "the world's only toaster with tête-à-tête controls."

I knew what he had to say right away—*projections off, rescinding job offer,* etc.—and I told him that he was a good man for calling me himself, rather than having some lackey do it. And I wished him the best of luck in the future, because I wanted to show him that I wasn't some dube who fell apart when he got bad news.

I let my mom know what had happened and went to my room and played the Electric Light Orchestra louder than usual. I know that it's supposed to be a sign of sensitivity that you can cry, but if I had cried on the phone with the home appliance executive, it just would have made him feel bad. If I had cried in front of my mom, she would have been scared and she's had enough to deal with ever since my Dad left when I was thirteen.

Then I reminded myself that we had a sign in the cross-country locker room in high school that said, "*Win with humility, lose with dignity.*" That's how I try to live my life.

But I couldn't help myself. I put my head in my pillows and turned up the stereo even louder and, suddenly, it was like an earthquake in my head but I just kept pressing my face into the pillow so I didn't disturb anyone and, when I was done, it was like someone had thrown a glass of water on the pillow.

When I walked out of the room, my mom was standing there and she pretended like she just happened to be passing by.

"I gotta get a sandwich," I said.

"Okay" is all she said and she looked at me and tried to touch my shoulder. You know how you sometimes get something on you and you squirm around to shake it off? Even though I was in my twenties, that's how I felt when Mom touched me. I ran down the stairs.

I got work as the assistant manager of the Nuts to You hardware store. The owner/manager had inherited Nuts to You from his dad and wasn't crazy about doing actual work, so he let me pretty much run the place. He gave me my own desk, which was cool. I liked the work I did—planning schedules, ordering inventory, putting up signs, talking to the customers. And working in a hardware store in a town like Minnisapa was like something in an old movie.

Jimmy Stewart is one of my role models. I cleared my desk every morning when I arrived, then drank the coffee and ate the donut I bought at the Go Mart across the street. And the hardware stuff itself was cool: the screws in little packets, the light bulbs in their corrugated packages, the displays of lawn mower and lawn tractor wheels; everything was silver and black and gray, and it had that hardware store smell, which is like drugstore smell only less powdery and more rubbery. Everything was solid; everything was practical; everything could be counted. But a hardware store in my hometown still wasn't where I was supposed to be.

One day, our cross-country coach came in. I heard the bell that signaled the door opening. He held the door for someone and yelled to me, "Hey, Slow, great to see your smiling face." The horrible thing about Coach is that he meant it.

"And good to see you, Coach Brum," I said. I knew I wasn't smiling. I could feel it in my face.

"I've been hearing great things about you," he said. "Something about an engagement and a job." It was almost a question, but not quite.

I had to just suck it up. "Unfortunately, both of those have fallen through."

He didn't say anything right away. Then he said, "That's really too bad. But it's good news for a guy like me, in search of a lawn mower wheel."

I was glad that he got off the subject. I tried to remember how he did it, so when I was older, I could do the same. But when the store was empty, I went to my office and put my head in my hands. I didn't cry, but I wanted to.

After work I'd walk for miles and miles and miles, stupid as a pinball. I'd think about Kelly and then try not to think about her.

But then I'd start to thinking about her or some other girl, and it wasn't like my normal girl thoughts where they had sex with me because they thought I was such a nice guy. The girls had sex with me kind of because they didn't like me and I was mean to them, in various ways I won't get into now. This was totally sub-wholesome, but I liked it and it wasn't just that I liked the sex fantasy, which you can't help but like. I liked being mean. When I talked to a priest about it at confession, he said that the church wasn't quite as rigid about impure thoughts as it used to be, and told me to simply pray that they be relieved. The jury is still out on whether they have been.

I'd walk for two, three, four hours at a crack. Once I got off work at four and walked until midnight. I covered close to thirty miles, walking and thinking and hardly even noticing what was around me.

And I kept running into this crazy nun, who'd gotten kicked out of the church. She'd ride around on a bicycle with these big garbage bags full of cans hanging from it. She told me that the devil loved me as much as Jesus did.

I was walking one night when I encountered the nun coming the other way on her old lady bike. She looked at me with these eyes which were both too there and too not-there at the same time. She looked at me and said, "Jesus raped me."

She moved past like a scene in a movie, where suddenly somebody's face is the size of a tidal wave and then it's nothing at all. She was trailing behind her the two big bags of crap that are tied to her bike. They were about as gross as stomachs.

I blurted out, "Jesus!"

Sometimes I'd stop in and see Chimes Sanborn at the bowling

alley. Chimes wasn't always as wholesome he should be, but he's nonjudgmental because being judgmental doesn't get you real far in the bowling alley business.

I played a lot of pinball. You play with your back to the bowling and, when you don't see bowling, but just hear it, it's like a storm at sea. And, all the while, I'm focused on the pinball game which has got Captain Kirk and two space babes on it. They are from a planet which developed bikini technology at around the same time Earth did. You always feel a little dube just playing this game 'cause of the near-naked girls on it. And I remember thinking, "I wonder what being on a pinball machine does for your ego? What's it feel like to be Shatner and walk into a bowling alley and see yourself with two space babes on a pinball machine?" That also raises the question of whether or not, when Shatner gets bored, he just goes bowling.

When I play pinball, I concentrate, because anything that's worth doing is worth doing right. I watch the ball as it falls and dings back-and-forth and settles into sockets. I nudge the machine just enough to affect its trajectory but not enough to tilt it. I try to let everything extraneous go and focus, like I'm still in high school and running a race in cross country. At times like this, the bowling alley is just an ocean and the sounds are just a storm and I am focusing on this game; it pings and darts and lights up. The ball droops down, and here's where I sometimes flub it. But I catch it on a flipper and send it back on to ricochet around some more for my greater glory. I scored extra balls on this game and then on a second game, but I lost focus and had five awful games in a row, and it just seemed sad that I'm banging this stupid ball around, and the next thing I knew it was two hours later. I focused and recovered; in fact, I got the highest score ever—or at least since the last time Chimes unplugged the machine to sweep—and I still had one ball left. But I left the free ball because I was embarrassed that I was twenty-five with a masters in engineering, and I was this good at pinball.

I sat at the counter, sipping my Diet Coke and eating Funyuns, watching people bowl. When people leave their group and grab their bowling ball and look at the pins, they get a look you don't usually see as people are backing out of parking spots and ordering Cokes and doing the other stuff that passes off as life. They quiet down and summon their inner resources and approach the lane and, after they release the ball, they keep watching, even though it's literally out of their hands. They watch the ball as it makes its journey across the lane. Then, unless they totally suck, the ball hits the pins, which scatter and fall and then that pinsetter thing makes everything all right again. This all prompted me to say to Chimes, "The cool thing about bowling is that knocking stuff over is the whole point." That was all I said because if I said the other stuff I was thinking, he'd say something like, "You're going soft on me, Slow."

At this point in my reverie, some kid came up to me.

"Aren't you going to use this ball?"

"No, go ahead. Knock yourself out."

"Thanks, man."

And then he said, "You're Jodie Slocum's brother. Weren't you getting married?"

Chimes looked at him and said, "Play the fucking ball." He's not supposed to say that because this is a customer, and saying "play the fucking ball" is less than optimal customer service, but he said it anyway because he understands loyalty. And, anyway, the kid was like sixteen and more or less expected to be yelled at.

I was sitting at the kitchen table with my mom, complaining about the nun I kept running into and her habit, so to speak, of making pronouncements about the Devil and Jesus. I didn't go into the details of the pronouncements.

"Honey, she's insane. She can't help it. The Diocese is trying to get her some help."

I'd never thought about what it meant to be insane. I always thought it just meant being an uber-dube. But then I thought that it must be like living in a cave filled with sleeping bats, and always being terrified that those bats would wake up, and, the worst part would be, you would never be able to leave the cave because it was the inside of your own skull.

One day in the early part of September, when other people were back at school, I realized that I'd been in Minnisapa for so long that even when I stepped outside for a walk it felt like I was inside. The hills just looked like somebody's grandma's ottomans. And when I stopped in the bowling alley and played pinball, it felt like I was actually inside the game. I couldn't breathe and I was way too far away from anything like fresh air. I told Chimes I was taking off and hopped into my car. I drove north up Highway 61 toward the Cities.

North of Minnisapa, I passed the place by the river where Chimes and Pooch and Smash Sanborn and Quint King and I would ride our bikes in the summers once we got old enough to ride our bikes outside of Minnisapa. Between the highway and the river, there was this piece of abandoned highway that ran parallel to the real highway, like a remnant of a lost civilization. It was kind of bleached and weedy. Then there was a railroad track between that and the river. The river didn't always smell very good, especially on those days in late August when the water was low and you'd occasionally find some fish who had botched the few life-decisions that fish are expected to make and had taken a wrong turn so it was rotting in what used to be a couple feet of water but was now only a couple of inches of water. The fish's white underside and scared eyes were something you weren't supposed to see. It was around that time of the year when our moms would look at each other and say, "They really should be getting back to school," the idea being that if we didn't get some new shirts and a sense of purpose, we'd go sociopath on them.

Our moms were on to something. Hanging out on an abandoned road by a backwater didn't exactly bring out the best in us. Sometimes we'd kill frogs. We wouldn't kill them for any reason, other than to show them who was boss, which I always assumed they already knew, given that we had all the technology. We would smack them or stab them with sticks. We wouldn't do anything with them after that. We'd just leave them lying there, more or less exploded, and even uglier than they were before they were killed. This was when my dad was still around, so I didn't have to worry so much about setting an example, and I had the freedom to act like a dube.

And then there was the time, just before fifth grade, that we were exploring a little north of where we usually hung out, maybe because we were depressed by all the murdered frogs around us. There was a triangle of skanky woods between the river and the railroad and we were walking around there when I noticed some of those emerald-colored glass things that they put on transformers. I've always thought those were cool, so we all started walking towards them. As we got closer it turns out that the transformers had been set there to mark somebody's stash of porn.

We were just figuring out about girls and that our parents had sex and what that might involve, and I was making the connection between that and the stiffness that would appear in my pants when the three girls threw their towels over the water tank in the opening to *Petticoat Junction*. I'd given up *Petticoat Junction* for lent that year, but didn't explain why to my parents. So you can about imagine the effect this porn had on a kid who was aroused by the opening of a TV show. This stuff was explicit, and it was covered with leaves and it had been rained on, which made it even more exciting. It wasn't just dirty pictures. It was somebody's secret.

We made some jokes, because we didn't really know what else to do. On the one hand, we were all really excited· and, on the other hand, we felt the way we felt when we saw the white underside of that dead fish.

As I drove north of Minnisapa, I reached the stretch before Red Wing where the radio doesn't come in. I turned it off, so the car was silent, other than the engine and wheel noises. I realized that I hadn't called my mom. I usually let her know what's going on, so she has one less thing to worry about. She would stay up when my younger brothers and sisters would stay out, or else she would go to bed with her face a little tighter than it should be. She never said anything, she just went into her room silently at about midnight.

I turned the radio back on and kept working the radio knobs until finally one of these guys who actually thinks of himself as "wacky" from Eau Claire or someplace was talking about a rockin' disco countdown. *It's 1984. Give it up, pal.* But then this probably isn't how he planned his life would turn out, either.

When I drove through Hastings, there was some guy with a pot gut and a T-shirt that said "Party Most Hardy" in big letters on the front, which evidently represented his life philosophy. I thought of how Pooch and I would talk about how we, first, hated people who used "party" as a verb and how we had thought that was the quintessence of dubeness, but that we had underestimated the talent of dubes for dubeness, because we hadn't seen the refinement of "party hardy" coming and then this guy took it up to even another level with the whole "most hardy" thing and then put it all on a T-shirt. But this guy had a girl on his arm.

When I got to the Cities, the freeways didn't do anything for my mood. One lane just ended, for no apparent reason, and I nearly got killed merging into the lane next to me, even though I'm a responsible driver. And then it started to rain, and I had the windshield wipers going a mile a minute. I wound up on some side street and saw these lame business signs like "Twin Cities Reptile" and "Twin Cities Janitorial Supply" which caused me to muse ironically on the superior retail offerings of a large city. I didn't know where the hell I was.

And then I saw a sign that was sort of toenail yellow that said, "Adult Movies." However lame Minnisapa was, at least it didn't have that particular temptation. But seeing that sign came at a really bad time, because I'd had plenty of unwholesome thoughts all the way up to the Cities, and I'd felt a kind of mean emptiness. I'd been a virtual paragon of level-headedness and clean living and chivalry and here I was, having last touched a female when my mom tried to pat me on the shoulder five months ago. But then, I reminded myself that *character is what you do when nobody can see you.*

But I did need to eat something and there was a bar that looked like it might serve a burger. So I parked the car and got out. The whole neighborhood felt nasty. There were no trees except for some skinny little things handcuffed to black poles and set in cedar

141

chips on the sidewalk. There were posters stapled to round poles. There were so many staples and tufts of poster that it seemed as if the staples were an insect which had swarmed and attacked the wood. From the punk posters that were still up, I figured that I must be close to the U.

I prepared myself for walking into this bar because, even in Minnisapa, walking into bars always kind of throws me. It was loud, and everybody was yelling over the music, and these clumps of people were in the booths, and they looked up until they realized I wasn't somebody they cared about, which is weirdly insulting, and then they looked suspicious and went back to their conversations which looked like people trying to act like they were in a beer commercial. Everything was hard to understand, and there was a pressure that there isn't to normal air.

And I noticed my buddy James T. Kirk, on the pinball machine, which cheered me up a little. But I kept walking to the bar, and sat down, but not next to anybody.

The bartender was about fifty, and he smiled and asked me how I was doing when I sat down. He looked like he might be from Minnisapa—grey hair, a happy potato face—and his name was Oscar, which is just a great old-guy name. He'd started bartending here when he was twenty-one and had worked as a busboy at the restaurant next door before that. Whenever somebody came up to order a pitcher, they made a big deal of using his name, like they were friends with a celebrity. He explained that the bar was more crowded than usual because tonight was the ending of softball season for a couple of teams that the bar sponsored. I knew he had a job to do, so I tried not to monopolize him.

But when he turned to serve another customer, it felt like the barometric pressure of the bar had increased around me again. I could barely breathe, with all the smoke in the air. I tried to sip my beer and look like I had some business here, which is surprisingly hard to do. I didn't spend a lot of time in bars in Minnisapa, but when I did it was to meet people, and I also usually knew some of the other people in the bar from school or something.

I noticed that there was a tiny Christmas tree next to the cash register and that it was decorated with tiny hardhats and lunch boxes. It was over three months until Christmas.

I was also a) trying to get up the nerve to go into that porn store and b) trying to talk myself out of it.

"So, Oscar, what's the deal with the Christmas tree?" I asked.

"Oh, that. I almost forget it's there. We keep it up all year and decorate it with whatever holiday we're closest to. That's for Labor Day."

At this point, I was out of conversation. This was excruciating. I should either walk up to the porn store or go home, either of which would be lame.

I ordered another beer to go with my burger and spent a lot of time kind of looking at it like those poor guys I used to see at dances who didn't have anyone to talk to and would like stare at a piece of the wall like it was a television program with special bulletins just for them.

Some girl came up to the bar and said, "Oscar, can I get a Leinie and quarters for pinball?'

She looked at me and went, "Hey." She was a girl I wouldn't normally have much interest in. She hadn't done anything with her hair and she wasn't wearing any make-up. She was wearing a jean jacket. She didn't belong to any of the groups in the bar.

I said, "hey" back to her and she said, "I forgot the place is filled with softball creeps tonight." And I agreed with her estimation of the clientele and, looking back at Kirk and the space babes, said, "that's one of my favorite pinball games."

She said, "Yeah, it takes my mind off things. You want to

play after I'm done?"

I was agreeing to this when Oscar came back with her change and her beer. I asked her how her day was, even though I know this isn't exactly a brilliant line. Still, she looked me in the eye, her own eyes went soft, and then she wobbled into me. She had whiskey or something on her breath and when she turned I saw a pack of cigarettes in the pocket of her jean jacket. "How was my day?" she asked, as if reorienting herself. "Oh, horrible. I just had to go to a work party where I really felt out of place. Everyone there hates me."

"You seem really nice to me," I said. She had, after all, spoken to me when no one else would. "Why would anyone hate you?"

"I don't know. Because I'm not like them." She lit a cigarette. I tried not to flinch. She drank half of the beer in one swallow and then just started talking to me about how she grew up in one of the fancier suburbs, which always felt like a party where she didn't know anyone. She told me her name was Gail.

I said, "I'm glad you showed up. Until you got here, the only person who was nice to me was Oscar."

She said, "Isn't Oscar great?" And I can agree with this, too, and then, not knowing what to say next, I looked away and straight ahead, at the bottles behind the bar. When I turned back, having thought to ask her what she does, she was finishing her beer.

She said, "I'm gonna play pinball now." And then she looked into my eyes and touched my arm and asked, "Are you gonna be here when I'm done?' in a way that implied she hoped I would be. When she walked over to the pinball machine, she staggered.

When she was playing pinball, I headed back to the bathroom, wading through the bar. When I closed the door, it became quiet. Some graffiti had been gouged into the wall so it looked like an asylum wall. Water condensed on a pipe just above the graffiti. There was a big rush of noise, and then some guy was standing at the urinal next to me. He asked, "Been partying pretty hardy?"

"Yeah," I said. "Pretty hardy."

When I got back to the bar, Oscar did a weird thing. He said, "I'm sorry. I forgot to ask for i.d." I'm four years over the drinking age and look totally responsible.

But he didn't give it a quick look. He stared at it for a while. He was being chivalrous. He was trying to remember my name and where I lived. I didn't meet his eye when he returned the wallet.

She came back. "I didn't do real well." I noted that she said "well," which is correct, instead of "good."

"I'm a little too loaded tonight," she said.

"Yeah, I know how that goes," I said, which might be vague enough to not be a lie.

She looked down at the bar, and announced, "I'm a witch."

I must have looked at her funny.

She continued, "But I don't, like, put spells on people to hurt them."

"Everyone has the right to protect themselves," I said and she looks up at me. Her eyes brighten, like I just said the one thing that explained her life.

She said, "You wanna go outside and smoke a joint?"

"Sure."

It had rained. The air was cool and quiet and clean, and she immediately walked close to me, so that my arm was just naturally around her, and we kissed before we got three feet from the bar. Some guy—I think the guy from the urinal—walked past and said, "Way to go, dude." I flinched, but I don't think she heard him. We kissed so hard that I could taste her cigarette smoke in my mouth.

"I live like two blocks from here, there's a shortcut I know," she said and I followed her behind a grocery store. It didn't smell good. They'd thrown out some produce or something. We kissed some more and then hopped up on a loading dock. She pulled out a joint and some matches and lit it up and took a drag.

She handed it to me.

"That's funny. You hold it like a cigarette," she said.

"Yeah, my friends make fun of me. But that's how I've always done it." She smiled. I felt like I was the Grinch and I successfully lied to Cindy Lou Who. The smoke burned and choked me, but I didn't let it show. It didn't do much for me.

When we were done with the joint, I realized that our legs were dangling a few feet off the ground. So I slid down and said, "Here, I'll help you down."

"Oh, thanks," she said. "My knight in shining armor."

But standing made all the beer and pot and cigarette smoke and general weirdness woosh through me and so when she said, "Here I come," I didn't quite make the connection and let her crash down. She hit her head on the way down and landed in a puddle. "Oh, God," I finally said. When I leaned to give her a hand up, her eyes flared anger at me, and she said, "You just let me fall!" and she waved me away. She crawled a couple of steps away and, still on her hands and knees, stared at the wet alley pavement. The light wasn't good, but her face looked like it was shaking, like she was going to cry. As she turned back around, she said, "Oh, God. How do I get into these things?"

I said, "Oh, I'm so sorry. Here, I'll help you."

But she said, "No, I can get up. No, I'm fine. Just stay away, please."

She got up. "I'm just gonna go home now," she said. "I'll be fine."

I thought I better respect her wishes. As she limped down the alley, I yelled, "I'm really sorry" at her, but she didn't say anything. She was crying, with big ripping sobs. I stood there until I saw her clear the alley.

I did what I had to do. I walked back into the bar and told Oscar what had happened and gave him my name and phone number and told him that I really enjoyed meeting Gail and asked him to let her know that. And then I drove home, stopping at an all-night place in Red Wing that served these insane German hash browns and huge Danishes and was always clean and friendly and where the waitresses always reminded me of the cafeteria ladies at school. They had new menus, and they printed the Ten Commandments on the back of each. I duly noted the irony, and called my mom so she could stop worrying.

WILDERNESS SURVIVAL

DESCRIBE WAYS TO AVOID PANIC AND MAINTAIN A HIGH LEVEL OF MORALE WHEN LOST.

Quint: The day is unresolved. It is a phrase from one of the old guys I drank with, one of the old guys I would probably someday become, and whom I weirdly admired. We were sitting there, insouciant as fetuses, floating in alcohol, when he said it: *The day is unresolved until I get to a bar.*

It is a weekday, just after work, and I'm standing in the aisle of a bus that is moving through downtown Minneapolis where, twenty-seven but just now out of college, I work as a project manager in a marketing firm. I'm grasping the overhead rail, shoved by everybody, smushed by everybody, harassed by these goddamn bus sounds—the sigh of the brakes, the ding of that cord that you use to request stops; I put up with this; I accommodate the push, strain, and sway, the various injustices of work rioting in my head, my suggestions dismissed because I am a mere project manager, the world reduced to this human cattle car, the horizon itching across the windows. The bus apparently crosses a bridge. Every moment is a waiting room for the next. The bus sways again and everyone leans into me again. Everyone jostles me. I feel like shit. I feel constricted, sour, touchy; I feel as if I have rubber bands rather than tendons in my forearms and chest. My chestbone clenches and tickles. I need a drink.

CR

This is one really fucking drunk taxi. The world is all opening and connecting, applauding and seeking, ghostly and volatile and dissolving.

I wound up in a weird bar in this nasty part of town. Northwoods murals on the walls, but you knew that everybody carried a knife. Some woman had given me a ride here, but she ditched me. I was her best shot at the previous bar. I wasn't her best shot at this bar. Old boyfriend or something. You know how that goes. I don't like this neighborhood. The windows here are all covered with boards or shattered into fangs.

The cab driver has an attitude, but I talk to him anyway. "Do you know that song, where the guy sings, 'And I ask myself how did I get here?'" The cabbie looks at how I'm dressed—still got my suit on, albeit worse for wear—and I can tell he's one of those immigrants disgusted by someone who would so squander his opportunities. Fuck him. "Fine, sorry to bother you. I'm just loaded." I sink back into the seat, and, even though we are still miles from my crappy apartment, I play a hunch. I reach into my back pocket to start to gather and count my money.

"I'm sorry. I just counted my money. I've got four bucks. Just pull over here." From the looks of it, my money has had an even worse night than I have. The meter says $3.80. "Here," I say, "I might have something for a tip." I don't wanna be a complete prick. I start to dig in my pockets. The cabbie says, "Do not bother, unfortunate sir."

So I stand here, at two in the morning on a Wednesday night. I have to be to work in six hours. I start walking, but I think that maybe, somehow, I've gotten turned around, and I'm not sure I'm going in the right direction.

CLIMBING

Slow: There were a number of ways this could have gone totally dube on me.

First, gravity. You see, Patricia and I would be sitting about ten stories in the air, in a swaying ferris wheel car, the sky in front of us, the ground under us, just a bar between us and tipping forward to our certain deaths. I'd done a test ride, by myself, with a fake ring. You could only do about a quarter turn inside the ferris wheel car and it was weird proposing to the air. And it had that quality of a rehearsal: softer, lighter, goofier, without the kind of traction that reality has. Some stresses and vectors missing. I'd thought of asking my Mom to do a test ride, but I thought I might as well invite Freud and then I thought of asking Pooch, who I heard was in town, but we would have needed to make about twenty nervous Gay jokes to get through first the proposal and then the slipping on of the ring and ever since Pooch's brother Darrin died of AIDS we're not making those jokes any more. (Of course, my plans for my engagement, which is the most hetereosexual and normal thing in the world, scooped up those memories and that guilt: it never occurred to me until I saw Darrin's body at the wake that, while the Bible says that homosexuality is a sin, it doesn't give the rest of us permission to make jokes at the expense of sinners and that the hundreds of fag jokes and nervous I'm-Not-Gay jokes and sissy jokes he heard in his twenty-two years on the planet probably did nothing to advance the cause of righteousness.) So, because fake-proposing to Pooch was out, I boarded the ferris wheel alone and, as it reached the top, I pivoted and declared my undying love to the rivets and the vinyl and the flanges 100 feet above Minnisapa and mimed sliding a crackerjack ring on a finger of air. At that height, the sky was like the regular air, only more charming and dangerous. I knew I might drop the ring, but the test ride gave me confidence.

Second, the carney. I paid the guy $25 and promised $25 more if he'd stop us at the very top, overlooking Minnisapa. At first, I was afraid of him, but I thought it was only polite to ask about his tattoos, and it turns out he treated them like pets. "This guy is from my hometown. This one reminds me of a girl I loved. This one was someone who stood up for me once." He pointed to—and then patted—a double star, a rose, and a bulldog.

Third, the concept. I'd made a list of supposedly cool ways to get engaged but they were like a dube highlight reel. Putting the ring in the cake seemed awfully close to a murder plot. Proposing on the Jumbotron at your local stadium seemed like something you did between beer belches and nachos and "We Are The Champions." I don't think any woman wants her moment to be interrupted by a bunch of guys saying, "Check it out, I'm on TV." I was looking for something a little more stylish. I usually ask myself what Ward Cleaver or Jimmy Stewart would do, but for this one I asked: What would Cary Grant do? I came up with handing her the ring at the top of a stopped ferris wheel as we looked over Minnisapa. If the sky and city could look like an early 1960s movie, that would be great, but I can't control that.

Fourth, me. I'd messed up an engagement before. The

moment you hand her the ring is supposed to be the moment when you affirm her completely. I'd screwed that up, when two-plus years ago I'd proposed to Kelly and insisted she go to confession. I thought I was being moral but I was being a dube. In the intervening time, I'd gotten either more realistic and tactful or I'd compromised my values, but, whatever happened to me, I wasn't going to start going on about purifying her sins. Frankly, she wouldn't put up with it. Patricia loved me, but thought I was a little full of it. She grew up on a farm with five other brothers and sisters and her mom and dad were still alive and together and her oldest brother took over the family farm and her other brother bought the farm next door and everyone came back for Christmas to the home place—that's what they called it, the home place—and I think, because of this prosperity of the heart, Pat always assumed what I never assumed: that things will be okay, that we don't need to make all sorts of crazy lists and to constantly judge our lives against some ideal of a wholesome, level-headed rich life. But she was also smart enough to know that I needed to do these things.

Fifth, the timing. We'd talked about a future together, so I wasn't surprising her. I was just saying the words—marry me—that hadn't been said.

Sixth, Acts of God: rain, tornadoes, the first ever monsoon in southeastern Minnesota, mechanical malfunctions, muscle spasms, spontaneous astigmatisms, some dube butterfly in Brazil fluttering its wings and messing everything up.

But I'd checked out everything I could check out and everything seemed okay. So here we were on a beautiful June night. You have to understand the particular nature of a beautiful night in June in Minnisapa, Minnesota because this isn't like a beautiful night in June in California. To understand June in Minnesota, you have to understand late October and November and December and January and especially February and March in Minnesota, when winter won't get up and move on, when winter gets depressed and stops combing its hair and washing its face, when you no longer think about how cool the geometry of snowflakes is or how cool the physics of skating is, and the air is essentially a psychopath you should not be spending a lot of time with, and then it's February and the snow looks like an ashtray and then it's March and you get more cold and blizzards so it seems that the forces of randomness and entropy are just showing off so you just shrug and show up for work and take your vitamins and try to work the rowing machine now and then and not be too much of a drag. And then around mid-April, which elides into May, this part of the planet starts to get it together; it starts to slowly warm and bloom; and then you have June and June is just so awesome and the world is green and the air is gentle. I like to think that happiness is the natural culmination of character building but sometimes it's just "Hey, I've been let out of prison." So as you park your car, and put your arm around your almost-fiancée, and approach the Minnisapa Days Midway, you chalk one up for photosynthesis as you step on the oxygenating grass and you thank the planet for tilting in such a way that you can roll up the sleeves on your oxford shirt and walk around at 9:00 at night in daylight.

We walked past the hot-dog-and-fries smell and the aggregating and competing human voices and the sound of generators and the sound of all sorts of things whipping around at high speeds and people screaming and the occasional dinging bell or carney pitch, past the shacks full of conscripted teddy bears and the weirdly zombie-like rubber ducks that bob and progress on that thin little strip of water and various simians trying to impress their womenfolk with Feats of Skill and Strength and the kids running around holding galaxy-like swirls of cotton candy. And, of course, everyone is out in this great weather and some of us are back in town, so we ran into my high school Cross Country Coach who beamed when he saw me and shook my hand and then Pat's hand and told her she was a lucky woman. Then we saw Duane Einwald who I made a point of calling Duane because in high school we had called by a different nickname every week. I have realized that much of what we thought of as funny was, in fact, mean and it is not Christian to treat people like punch lines. Turns out he's doing great, that he's an art director in a Twin Cities ad agency which sounds totally cool and that what we thought was a little talent at art was really a passion and gift. We evidently missed a lot when we were wisecracking. Then, almost inevitably, Dickie Burpee appears, wobbly drunk, bulked up, in an auto repair shirt, from the beer tent; he's back from the army with his girlfriend and he introduces me as "his friend, Slow Slocum" and shakes my hand for a little too long and I talk about how we go way back and ask about the army which I think is a great institution for beating the dubeness out of people. Then he says, "The four of us should really get together." And I say, "Sure. We don't get to Minnisapa much, but let's try to do that."

This is kind of a lie and I don't think it's snobbism to say we won't ever get together. Dickie's a good guy but I can tell his idea of getting together is partying and I don't acknowledge the verb form of "party."

Still, Pat looks up at me like, "We're not going to" and I say, "No, it's never going to happen. Just small talk."

Other than these glitches, Minnisapa was being awesome. We met like five other people I knew from school.

And Minnisapa was being hilarious. We'd stopped at the bowling alley and Chimes Sanborn had brightened when I walked in and he made a big deal out of greeting me. He said to Patricia, "This is a straight arrow guy. I would trust him with my life." Chimes didn't tease me or do one of these "oh, watch out for this son-of-a-bitch" kind of things. But then Patricia said, "And he's less boring than he seems . . . he's kind of stealth interesting" which made Chimes snort. Chimes asked if we would be listening to the fireworks on the radio, which you can actually do. Minnisapa might be a joke, but it's a can-do joke. It's a joke committed to innovation. This year, the owner of the radio station was broadcasting from a milk carton boat. But, no, we'd be seeing the fireworks live.

As it was getting dark, and the fairground lights were deepening against the sky, I suggested to Pat, with that abruptness that comes when you've rehearsed something too much, "Let's go on the ferris wheel, it'll be cool to look out over the town." But she said, "sure" and I signaled the carney when we got on, and he winked almost too obviously back at me. As we sat in the rocking ferris wheel car, the anticipation of the ride, which normally wasn't much, and the anticipation of the proposal, which was plenty, all mixed and frothed inside me. And then the ride started up we ascended and we saw first the lattice work of the wheel filtering the night sky and then as we approached the top, the air sort of participated in our stomachs, and we saw the hills without obstruction, dark except for a few lights, and then the dark lake. I was surprised at how much of Minnisapa was massive and unlit. But, below us, we saw the golden, glowing smudge of the midway and the miniaturized people and the spreading grid of lights of Minnisapa. It was very cool and I knew this was going to be awesome. Pat was talking about how she wanted to ride a ferris wheel in a really big city and going on some about how I was evidently Mr. Popular and asked if I paid all those people to pretend to be my friends to impress her. I wasn't saying much, because I was getting nervous. Then, the second time around, we stopped at the very top, and I worked the ring out of my pocket, and turned and said, "Pat, I love you and I will love you forever." She could see what was coming as I turned and got the ring out and ready to slide onto her finger. Her eyes widened and she half-smiled, half started to cry, and I asked, "Will you marry me?" And she said yes and we kissed as best we could and the illuminated night effervesced through us and around us and we looked down upon the lights below like the King and Queen of a small but very cool kingdom and when we swooped past the operator, I gave the carney the thumbs up. Making the next passes was cool, although I had to keep nodding at the carney. Pat said, "A part of me just wants to wedding plan and project manage. But I know I should just shut up and enjoy this" and she tucked in closer to me. Then when we left, I shook the carney's hand and slipped a twenty and a five in there, and as we stepped down the stamped metal ramp with the big rubbery cords underneath, we walked into the crowd and although I know that the crowd's composition was half simian and/or dube, it felt as if I briefly saw what Jesus always saw and I realized that every soul was ecstatic and luminous and worthy and every created thing was ecstatic and luminous and worthy, and while that is in some ways not level-headed, it is the truth, and I held Pat even closer as, together, we walked into the night.

FIRST AID

DESCRIBE THE SYMPTOMS, PROPER FIRST AID
PROCEDURES, AND POSSIBLE PREVENTION
MEASURES FOR HYPOTHERMIS; CONVULSION;
FROSTBITE; BRUISES, STRAINS, SPRAINS . . .

Chimes: I attended one class at Minnisapa State. Marketing 101. And in that one class, I learned one thing. Coco Chanel, showing amazing insight for someone named Coco, said it about perfume, but it goes for bowling. "In the factory, it's perfume. In the store, it's hope." Bowling alleys aren't about bowling. We've got the best bowlers in town here at the alley. And maybe two guys out of a hundred can actually tell the difference between a lane which is maintained to professional standards and the kitchen floors that other alleys pass off as a lane. I am not in the bowling business. I am in the friendship business. And that is why I wound up at Burpee's for the Super Bowl. That, plus we've got history. Burpee used to hang with our crowd in grade school and j-high. Back then, everybody was an idiot. Dickie just stayed there.

It was way the hell over in Wisconsin. Up on some ridge in a farmhouse he rented. Fucking middle of nowhere. A little too *In Cold Blood*. Not my kind of place. I like a Go Mart within six blocks. Burpee said he liked the place because he could party all he wanted and not bother anyone.

The place had that old-people smell from the previous tenants. Smelled like Campbell's Soup and mothballs. Burpee was drunk already. His girlfriend was drunk already. I don't think the game had started yet. There were maybe two other guys there. Not exactly the social event of the season. So I was glad I showed up. My job is to make people feel like they have more friends than they do.

I only stayed for the first quarter because a) I had other engagements. b) I didn't want to be driving too much up here on those hill roads and c) Burpee had the classic signs of late-stage smashed: Talking to himself and the entire room at once, despite the fact that none of us were actually listening. Forgetting what he just said. Repeating what he just said. Missing the most obvious clues to shut up. This included the phrase, "Shut up, Burpee." Insisting on grabbing you by the arm and looking you in the eyes when he said something. Smelling like a gas tank with the cap off. Farting without realizing it. Swaying so damn much you wanted to lay down bets on whether he would take out the onion dip or the lamp when he fell.

Burpee decided to deliver a speech on the coin toss, of all things. And, he had like an hour's worth of material on this topic. He was talking about how when he was a kid he even made his little plastic football game men shake hands. How the coin toss was an affair of honor, opposing warriors shaking hands, blah, blah. Blah. And then he got all nostalgic and went on about other relics of our misspent youth, like Creepy Crawlers and Incredible Edibles and other things where you heated up plastic goop in trays. Football in the street. Four-square. Kickball. Jiffy Pop on Friday nights.

And then he went on about the Packers, who he viewed as guardians of all that is good and true. He knew everything that Vince Lombardi ever said. He was driving his girlfriend nuts. She kept saying, "Dickie would you shut up and let our guests get a word in," and he said, "Yeah, just one more thing," and he would repeat for the third time "the frozen tundra of Lambeau field." I have been privy to some spectacular rants, but this wasn't a rant. This was something else. I left when he was launching into something about how Super Bowls should be played in the cold. He was going on about the Ice Bowl of '67 when his beloved Packers beat the Cowboys and everyone froze their nuts off. He was saying how cold tested character.

I walked out at about the same time that his girlfriend did. She was seriously pissed off. She had a bottle of schnapps with her and I said, "Are you gonna be okay?" And she said, "Yeah I just need some air." She swayed and righted herself. I pointed out that it was pretty damn cold for a stroll. She said it was preferable to dealing with Dickie when he was like this. She seemed like an all-right broad. He'd met her in the service, and she'd actually fallen in love with the little son-of-a-bitch. You have to admire that. Not everyone gets Burpee.

She walked out into the fields. Middle of fucking January. Zero and dropping. I should have added two plus two.

According to a police source of mine who stops by the bowling alley, her footprints indicated that she'd fallen down one of the little inclines behind the barn where it headed down to the pasture. She was so drunk she thought it was a good idea to go to sleep. There were cuts on her face, but there wasn't any foul play. By that time of year, the old snow thawed and refroze to form a layer of ice on top so when she fell through it, it cut her face. Burpee didn't have a mean bone in his body. He cried in high school when he hit Barb Carimona with an orange.

Dickie didn't know anything was up until the next morning. I can guess how he must have felt. He woke up and his head felt like a fist squeezing a rubber ball and, even though there hadn't been many people there the place looked like it had been broken into.

He yelled her name some because he didn't want to be bothered to get off the couch, not with his head feeling like that, but no one answered. Then he went to their room and the covers were exactly as they had left them the day before. And then he got sick to his stomach. He saw her small footprints head away from the house.

SAFETY

MAKE A PLAN FOR ACCIDENT PREVENTION
PROGRAMS FOR FIVE
FAMILY ACTIVITIES OUTSIDE THE HOME . . .

Quint: I quit drinking like six weeks ago, and you know how that goes. I feel like a kid again, and that's a less pleasant condition than you might imagine. Kids are scared a lot. Kids don't know what they're doing.

But there's something to just waking up with a clear head and a more-or-less clear conscience and seeing that I have plenty of time to get ready for work and being grateful for the stupid couch cushion which I use as my bed, and there's something to seeing my roommate's sherbet-colored cat who's wondering what the hell I'm doing up at this time of the morning and who ignores me when I try to give it some affirmations. I consider it a huge fucking deal that I'm not filled with panic, other than the panic that accompanies breathing, and that there aren't any hungover capillaries fluttering in my brain, and that there's nothing wrong with me that taking a hot shower and drinking my coffee and having a cigarette—I get a lot done in the shower—and saying my stupid prayers won't improve. In fact, there's a second here where I'm staring at the brown soap sliver in the little wire thing that hangs from the showerhead and everything clarifies. I have my own little personal haiku right there, staring at the soap sliver.

Then I get dressed and walk out into the cold air and really feel it and breathe it deeply and scrape the frost from my windshield and notice the hatchings of clear window and watch my breath appear and dissipate and listen to the car's engine idle and the smoke stream from the muffler and notice all the other shit that only a recovering alcoholic would consider a spiritual experience. I see other people starting their own cars and creating their own little clouds, and think "It's a party." I'm too bundled to wave and not awake enough to really care so I just shrug "hello."

I'm immensely happy because I know that I will be on time for work. I've started out early because my racing heart wakes me up these days and because I'm making up for lost time. But even if I were late, it would be regular-people late, not the epic, absurdist late of my unfortunate past, not showing up two hours late in the clothes you wore yesterday and realizing when you duck into the bathroom at the earliest opportunity that you hadn't been fully successful in washing the vomit out of your hair.

Like I said, I feel like a kid, with all that implies, so the whole scene reminds me of winter in Minnisapa. I mean, remember when snow was pretty much just an art supply, like those stubby scissors and construction paper and the dried little pond beds of watercolors? And when you came trudging home from supper with the snow jammed down in your boots and all melty and your face stinging a little from where somebody had nailed you with a snowball and everything just seemed to make your house even cozier, how you could see the kitchen light on and your mom moving around? My family loved coziness, especially when my dad was still alive. He was a nut for it. He'd run fans in, like, December so that he could pile on blankets and feel even cozier.

And when the snow really fell, it was like a vast note

excusing me from school and it glowed like a book I hadn't read. And there was this absolutely pure sense of holiday when the radio announced "Snow day!"

I remember how on snow days I would sit in the front room with my dad, who was a little cavalier about going into the office, and maybe even my brother and sister, and watch the snowplow pass, like it was our own private parade. The plow had a butterscotch-colored beacon that was multifaceted like the eye of an insect and when it would slide past our living room, scraping the snow ahead of it like surf, the entire front room would fill with its revolving light. I would feel enclosed in light. I will never forget that. In fact, I remember it just about every day.

I know my childhood wasn't as simple as I remember it. Or at least that's what people tell me here in soberland. And I know that everything changed by the time Dad died and Mom got scared and mean. But Minnisapa really had been sheltered. My standard line is that I'm burdened with a happy childhood, which gets laughs. I hear other people talk about their dysfunctional families and I kinda envy them. It's just me and my dysfunctional self.

I took buses for five years because I'd wrecked a car and hadn't ever quite gotten around to getting another. But now I'm driving again. I'm idling in the entrance ramp to the freeway just like a normal person, noticing how filthy the snow is on the side of the road. The line isn't too long; it's early. The heater strains to keep my windows clear. Condensation keeps forming on my side window, which bothers me, 'cause I have to see through that window to merge. I wonder if opening the windows would help or hurt, but having missed that class, I don't know. So I just smudge the window clear with my sleeve.

The freeway I'm entering snakes from Saint Paul to

Minneapolis and then continues into the suburbs and the marketing firm in the office park where I work. I hate freeways: The way they just ruin everything around them, this dirty snow, the way they bring out the asshole in everyone, like the punk behind me who thinks I haven't nudged ahead quickly enough. This idiot doesn't understand that the amount of space between me and the car in front of me has got next to nothing to do with when either of us gets on the freeway, that it is a matter of sequence, not space. I explain this to him by flipping him off.

It occurs to me that freeways are like a drug, but not one of your more interesting drugs, more like a combination of Novocain and speed, numb and nasty. Every day starts with a half-hour of anonymous hostility, which can't be good for the soul. If I had my druthers, I would rule a world filled with hot-air balloons and bicycles and trains. But this is the world I've been handed and I've been told that my tendency to create fantasy worlds is a part of my problem.

That said, nothing feels better than right now, when the entrance ramp light drops to green and I press down on the accelerator and merge into the traffic flow. That is one impressive little charioteer moment. The freeway has a nice contour to it, like a rope that's been snapped but not quite straightened, like some inspired engineer somewhere said the hell with the ruler and drew a beautiful freehand curve.

Twin Cities radio sucks, so I spend half my time, when I'm supposed to be driving, hitting buttons with my gloved hand, hoping to find something. Finally, I find a college radio station that plays something good, something from the time when I should have been in college but when I was, in fact, serving a four-year sentence in the navy. On a drunk, I'd befriended some college boys and I'd wound up on a campus somewhere on Chesapeake Bay and I remember walls lined with butcher paper filled with crayon drawings of some East German punk-rock singer, and there were Twinkies and milk on a table with what I assume was irony since everyone was drunk on their ass, and girls danced like dervishes and threw their hair, and this song played. *Some woman in a phone booth, not taking no for an answer, "hanging on the telephone."* One of those moments that stay in your mind like a snow globe, with nothing on either side of it.

The distance to the car in front of me narrows, so I brake.

The moment becomes a horrible room. The car is shooting across lanes, like a car on an amusement park ride, only it's not connected to anything. My guts lighten. The guardrail approaches, like all gravity got relocated there. Fuck. I spin the wheel but it's pointless. The car crunches and pivots and starts to skate, ass-backwards now, across the freeway, blurring the dawn, smearing the headlights of the approaching cars. I swear I see panic in those headlights; I swear they flutter and open up; it's like I suddenly discovered that every machine in the world had a living being in its center.

The retaining wall on the other side of the freeway approaches. This time I anticipate it, so it's worse. And, again, thud. I come to rest on the shoulder of the road, seemingly okay, the radio still blaring my private party. I turn it off and watch the traffic approach. It appears to have calmed down. I check to make sure that I am out of traffic. I think I am, but who knows. I think it's best to sit tight. I want to cry. I light a cigarette.

I hate the cars that go past now. They're a different kind of threat. They're an audience.

When the fuck did this become winter? When did gray skies and gray snow and killing yourself trying to get to your cubicle become winter? Winter had been a hell of a lot nicer in Minnisapa, when I was a boy and the town was protected by hills that always reminded me of kneeling buffalos. I wish I were there now.

When I was a kid, I think I loved ice even more than I loved snow. One Thanksgiving, we hadn't gotten any snow yet but the lake had frozen solid, so all of Lake Minnisapa was our skating rink. (Lake Minnisapa wasn't really a lake, just a channel of the Mississippi that somebody had blocked off by flipping over a barge.) Dad decided it was a good time to teach me to skate, since we had the whole lake. He was a great skater, though he was totally uncoordinated at just about everything else—badminton, softball, operating heavy equipment. And it was amazing to see him when he had the whole, glassy-grey lake to skate on, and not some crowded, chopped-up little rink. He was in a good mood, because the Friday after Thanksgiving was always his favorite day, anyway. He said it had all of the good parts of a holiday without any of the obligations. He took me to the far end of the lake, where we were sheltered by trees and swamp grass. I was seven.

"What do you skate on?" he asked me.

"My feet."

"No, what surface?"

I knew it was a trick question, but I had no idea what the trick was. So I answered it so he could make his point. I'm no dummy. "The ice."

"No, it only looks like you skate on ice. You actually skate on water." He twirled. "See here. The blade melts the ice when it touches it and creates water that you glide on."

I looked at a signature of water.

"Cool," I said, amazed at this subtlety and science that's

beneath our feet.

Every time I fell and skidded across the ice and felt the ice melt and soak into my clothes, I remembered what he had said. My toothy skates would flop out like flippers and I'd fall and look at the ice while I skidded. You could sometimes see leaves and weeds embedded in it. I went home that night ecstatic at this new angel skill, and looking as bruised as if I had been beaten.

Dad died when I was thirteen. That's when I stopped liking winter. That's when it lost whatever made it special. That's when I stopped skating and sledding and building snowmen. My life felt empty and cheap, like I was an athlete who retired and realized he wasn't good at anything else. Childhood had been my sport.

My memories of winter in high school were different—late February, early March, filthy slivers of snow, spongy yards, gray skies like particularly hopeless books. Friends of mine would take acid to make all those go away, for sheer Crayola effect, but I was too scared. I wasn't afraid of the drug. I was afraid of my fucking mind; I was afraid I would detonate some self-destruct sequence, some infinite regression, some mind-venom that I could never escape. Gray skies that you breathed into your bones were better than that.

I just spent hours in my room listening to records. Records are antiques now, with their beautiful labels, and the way they moved at the pace of a river, and that little riot of sound when you put the needle down, and the abyss at the center that the threads dropped into. They, too, are a part of my lost world. Now, we digitize our sadness.

My dad was a lawyer who did a lot of work for the railroad and some other transportation clients—barges, shipping companies, that sort of thing. I think I was the only ten-year-old in Minnisapa who knew what force majeure was. It's Latin for an "act of God," but what it really means is that something happened so unexpected that you can't be held responsible for it. When I claimed it as an excuse for not turning in my homework, my third grade teacher was pretty impressed, too. The sad thing is that wisecrack was the intellectual highlight of my life.

Our house was just a couple of blocks from the cinnamon-colored depot. It had the only vending machines where you could get Blackjack gum. Dad loved the fact that he could walk there, just like he could walk to his office downtown.

When we wanted to go on vacation, we would just hop on a train. Dad walked like a king on the train because he could get us little favors—extra bottles of Grape Nehi or Squirt; access to the engineer's car; a special audience with the porter, who had a story for every mile. I loved the way the train dignified everything it passed, even the loading docks and the old laundry lines in the back of people's houses, the way it made everything untouchable and incredibly vivid. It was like the world outside was already a memory. When we arrived at our destinations, we grabbed cabs and let them carry us through the city, to keep the feeling of flowing alive. Nobody in our family smoked—I picked up my habit on the street—but our living room was filled with ash trays from the places we had been—the Space Needle, the Saint Louis Arch, the Empire State Building.

I hold so tight to my memories because, if I lose them, they're gone, because the rest of my family really doesn't give a shit about that kind of thing. My dad actually disdained what he called merely personal history. When he was alive, you couldn't swing a dead cat in our house without hitting a multi-volume history of the Civil War in New Jersey or the memoirs of Napoleon's nephew twice removed, but you couldn't find a single photo album. Dad didn't believe in them. He thought they were vain; he thought they were symptoms of the decadent modern age. God only knows what he would think of me, playing the same memories over in my head every day, nursing the same regrets, reliving the same grudges, wondering why life isn't as charismatic as the movies. Why it is so dilute and dull.

The strange thing is that, although Dad never talked about the past, he kind of wore it around him, like an aura. He wore slightly beat-up suits with handkerchiefs in the pocket and he worked in an old downtown office with dark wood and those green-visored lamps everywhere. There was always something ghosty about him, something elegant and distracted. He kept falling over—in fact, that's how he died, falling off a barge—but he always made it seem as if the world was clumsy, not him.

I did hear one story about my childhood from the guys at the depot. Evidently, I had been a difficult baby and when I woke up for my first Christmas, not even two months old, I was particularly ornery, and I cried and cried, so, not knowing what else to do, Dad took me to the depot and we boarded a train going to the Cities. The moment the train began to move I stopped crying. All the way up to the Cities and back, the movement of the train lullabied me. Dad held me all that Christmas Day and we looked out at the flowing hills and trees and towns.

Between my dad's railroad connections, and the fact that his relatives were all dead and Mom's were all nearby, we were spared most of the cross-country car trips that other people suffered through. That was fine with me. Dad was graceful on trains, but peevish in a car. Although it was your basic 1960s boat, our car felt like it was some sort of experiment to see how we would react to cramped space. In fact, my only real memory of my parent's fighting took place in that car. Mom would second-guess Dad. Dad would snap back. Once, when we were driving to my uncle's farm near the Iowa border, Dad actually stopped the car and got out when Mom suggested that we back up and take a turn we'd missed, which had the fatal flaw of being right. Dad slammed the door and walked along the side of the road where the pale rock had fallen after they had sliced the limestone hills to cut this road. He walked straight ahead, never turned back, covered a good quarter mile before Mom realized he wasn't gonna stop. Mom slid over into the driver's seat and drove until she caught up with him and then leaned way back over the seat again and rolled the window down. He looked forward. She leaned and slid and contorted.

"Stop."

He kept walking. She had to slide back and drive forward again.

"Stop or I'll run you over."

He spun. "Don't talk to me when I'm trying to drive!" I'd never seen him so mad, and he wasn't even mad at any of us really, so we couldn't do anything. We just watched him sizzle like a monster. He marched around the car and got behind the wheel. Mom had to slide back again.

"Don't talk to me when I'm trying to drive. I've got enough in my head."

"We missed a turn, Henry," Mom tried to explain. She was mad and stubborn and almost crying.

"I don't care."

"I was trying to be helpful."

"I still don't care."

Dad drove the car up the hill, turned into a farm driveway, and backed onto the road. A pick-up blared its horn at him and swerved, spewing up the dust on the corner of the road. "Where the hell did he come from?" Dad asked. "Fuck him." He pounded the dash. Mom flinched.

We had never heard him say "Fuck" before. No one said anything for the rest of the ride.

I see the cop coming, flashing his little revolving light which looks like a miniature dawn. He shuts the siren off, but leaves the beacon flashing and spinning, which makes everything just that much trippier. He's skinny, with a kind of hangdog face. "You all right?"

Another trick question. My brain doesn't work, like a motor that's been flooded. I just kind of breathe, "Ah." Then I say, "Yes, officer. I'm fine."

"You probably feel a little shaken up."

"Yes, I believe I do." I don't know why I talk Southern to cops. They seem to like it, though.

I feel the urge to talk more, but silence keeps flowing in between the words. Silence is quicker than me. Then I say, probably stupidly, "I don't know what happened. I just lost control of the car."

"There's a lot of black ice here," the trooper says.

"Sorry?" I say.

"When it gets cold, all that exhaust you see streaming from the mufflers"—he points to the traffic—"freezes when it hits the road. You get enough cars passing over one spot, it can get pretty slick."

"Oh," I say. My mind makes a few grindings as if to elaborate and say something, something that a normal person might say, but thinks better of it. Then I think that if I had not wasted five years of my life in bars, if I had not just started driving again, I would know that.

"Is this address correct?" he asks.

"Oh, no. It's not, sir," I say. It is the address of the crappy apartment I'd lived in up until recently. It had been in one of those cheap square brick buildings for people who don't give a shit. It hadn't been much more than a place to crash, a "Free Parking" on my private monopoly board that otherwise was filled with various bars, a place I visited to sleep or suffer through a hangover. After I trashed the couch—or maybe it just fell apart, I don't know—it was just the couch cushion and some books and a cheap-ass stereo and I think maybe a fork and a glass with a caveman on it from Arby's. I called it minimalism. My real home was the bars where I went every night and bullshitted with the other regulars and percolated my resentments. Most of the other regulars were older than me. In fact, most of them were about the age my father was when he died. Hmm.

The cop hasn't just taken this opportunity to replay his entire wasted life. He says, "Make sure you get the address changed." But he's cool enough, though. He doesn't see any need to add one more fuck-up to the day, so he just gives the card back to me. He pivots it between his knuckles like he's doing a card trick. I'm amazed at this little bit of elegance in the cold on the freeway.

My car is pretty banged up. It looks like the whole left side is gonna have to be replaced. The door sags when I open it but it works and the car starts. I've got enough juice going through me from the accident that I'm not scared but I don't trust myself, so I drive like an old lady. When I walk into our suburban office complex, someone notices my car and says, "Get into an accident?"

"No," I say. "I ordered it that way."

Things stay weird. I spill some coffee on some office papers and, rather than just throwing them out, I hold them over the wastebasket so I can watch the ink run. I pay a lot of attention to the creaks in my body. Things buzz a little more than usual, which is never a good sign. My body becomes very interesting in a very uninteresting way. People stop by my cube and tell me about times in which they have spun across freeways for no good reason. Evidently there are cars out there careening around all the time. I just hadn't noticed. When it becomes clear that I'm not going to get anything done, I tell the department assistant that I'm leaving early to get estimates.

I wind up in a repair shop in a neighborhood close to my apartment that I've somehow never been in before. The streets in this part of Saint Paul remind me of Minnisapa. The houses are modest and, for that matter, so are the lawns, and they clearly don't get all uptight that there is an auto-repair place or laundromat on the block. The body shop has all this weird stuff in it—bas relief faces of pirates, in blue and red and tan paint. It's the kind of paint where they put it on a little too thick, so it bubbles and pocks like housepaint. Someone had once found these goofy painted heads somewhere and said, "Of all the things in the world, those are what I want to put on my wall." The heads had traveled from a factory somewhere to here, although I can't imagine how. There is an old rotary phone under a fold of old green foam insulation. The whole place is a randomness sandwich. Myself included. I look the pirates in the eye and say, "So how you guys doing?" at the precise moment the owner walks in with the estimate.

When I drive back from the auto body shop, the car creaks when I turn. My body creaks. My mind creaks. I'm up a creek without a paddle. It occurs to me that all this hurt and fogginess and anger could be elegantly resolved by a beer. Then I remind myself that what starts out as an elegant night around the glimmering bar always winds up with me sleeping in my piss in a Burger King parking lot and I'm in no mood to be pitied by a Burger King manager, so I say a little prayer to the God of My Understanding. I hate this. I hate this because the whole idea of a God of My Understanding is the theological equivalent of children's aspirin. The way I see it, God is a lot of things, but he's not customizable. You can't order the sun roof and the air conditioner. God is God. So there's a good possibility that I'm just making this shit up.

I actually affirm myself for going and getting estimates and driving home like a sissy rather than doing what I want to do, which is head straight to a bar and drink until I inhabit, for a couple of hours, that holy gliding place between dryness and disaster.

Affirming myself for doing an errand. Who knew that truth would be this dorky?

At the apartment, the cat ignores me and nothing else moves or soothes me, everything is quiet and still and empty, and I look at the bruise-colored sky and my bashed-in car. The prayer hasn't worked particularly well. I'm still feeling all fizzy, all tight and wrong and misaligned. And lonely. Nothing in the room is going to make me feel better.

I pray again. I pray like I mean it. I pray to the diffuse, difficult God of my understanding. I pray looking out at my gnarled car. I pray until the gnarls in my mind loosen and lighten.

I call Mom to let her know what happened.

"All day long," I say, "I felt just like Sylvester the Cat after Tweety Bird smacked him on the head with the frying pan."

"Is that one of those shows you kids used to watch?" she asks. Oscillating cats didn't play much of a role in her childhood.

"That's right. You didn't see a putty cat."

She ignores me. She sometimes gives the impression that

humor was a luxury we couldn't afford. "You're lucky, Quint," she says. "It could have been worse. You could have killed someone."

"Jesus, Mother. Don't be so melodramatic."

"I'm not being melodramatic." She's mad and stubborn, like she was in the car that time that Dad missed the turn. "Your father killed a little boy when he first started driving."

This hits me. I mean it hits me. I mean my brain cells flinch and flutter and a kind of electricity buzzes where thoughts are supposed to be.

"What? Why didn't I know about this?" My dad had been raised in upstate New York, the only son of parents who died before I was born. He had never returned there.

"That's not something you tell your ten-year-old son. It happened when he was just learning to drive. He'd swerved to miss a dog and hit the little boy who was chasing the dog."

She keeps talking, but I can't get it together to listen anymore; the words just become sound the way sometimes words on a page just become ink. My mind is slippery and somewhere else.

When I formalize my not-listening by hanging up the phone, a tone sounds. I have a message. I press the sequence of buttons. A voice from work tells me that I've missed a meeting. I try to listen but don't catch it. I sense the atoms vibrating in my body; I sense an effervescence where my flesh divides and divides until it becomes spirit. I pace the floor, not sure what its molecules might become, not sure of what is ice and what is water.

I replay the message, looking out the window at my wrinkled car.

It begins, "Where in the hell are you?"

Good question.

WATERSKIING

Barb: In the rearview mirror, I glimpse the ghastly beginnings of the bruises. I can feel the slight hum of their tenderness. Behind me is snoozing Chicago. It's been a mile since I've seen another car. I look down from the rearview mirror as a hamburger bag ascends like a hawk toward the windshield. I flinch and touch the brake. My ankle aches. The bag bounces on the hood of the Nova and tumbles up the windshield glass. Then, a pointless red light. Three in the morning, doors locked. All my possessions are in the trunk and backseat. My old suitcases, my overstretched laundry bags. My life is lumpy. The luggage my parents and aunts and uncles gave me when I went to college is no longer new, but I am too poor to buy new stuff. My car, my mom's old Nova, looks like a garbage scow. I'd packed it quickly. The city simmers around me. I look down, I don't know why. There's a frozen yogurt dish from a time we—the man who hit me, me—drove to a mall in the suburbs to shop; our afternoon in the suburbs was a kind of *naughty adventure* because we were supposed to hate the suburbs; there is also some flyer some religious nut had handed me and which my recently dumped boyfriend grimaced at me for taking; and then the matches that I used up in the car because I wasn't supposed to smoke in the apartment. Chicago feels more like a machine than a city. Bricks, concrete, the scaffolding of the El. Metal grates snarl in the business windows. The sweat which formed as I lugged everything to the car and is now drying. The dust which my packing stirred up has settled on me. My ankle hurts because I strained it lugging a suitcase down the steps of our apartment building.

The stoplight, having teased me enough, releases me. I enter the freeway heading north. After I threw up on Pooch's kitchen counter, and the guys walked me home, I never thought that I would be returning to Minnisapa for anything but visits.

My ankle throbs. The metaphor for love should not be the heart, but tendons. They are vaguely gristlely, like love. They connect us to the world. They are easily strained.

Tendons are the metaphor for my heart because they are graceless and everywhere.

Oh, my dear, I give you my heart. **Wrong.**

Oh my dear, I give you my ligaments, my cartilage, these stupid rubber bands in my ankles and elbows.

The freeway gurgles under the car. A zillion warehouses slur past. I think to switch on the radio. The bodacious FM, the black station I loved and he hated. There's no funk where I'm going.

The music gives out and I find the usual stupid classic rock. "The point of no return." Please. I don't even want an ironic relation to Journey or Foreigner or whoever these lameoids are, so I drive in silence. I zoom past the flat fields of Illinois then Wisconsin. Wisconsin's a little more interesting, but not by much. I can sense farmhouses along the side of the road. The yardlights glow. The farmhouses glow as the lights in their kitchens are turned on. Dawn approaches. The sky lightens in front of me.

By the time it is light I feel that I can pull over. I spot one of those gas stations off the freeway that rise up like lighthouses. When I go into the gas station, which is also a convenience store, I tell myself that a woman who has been hit by her boyfriend, and then broken up with him, and decided the sensible thing to do was to leave the apartment in the middle of the night, shouldn't have to worry too much about eating a proper dainty amount. I won't be dating much, soon, anyway. I feel as liberated as a little girl who just wants to buy candy. I seize a bagful of absolute crap. The awkward kid behind the counter looks at me like he might ask me something.

I say, because what have I got to hide anymore and because I have this dangerous urge to crystallize the discomfort in the room: "It's exactly what you think it is. The man I'm living with beat me, so I'm driving home to Minnesota." He is shocked by "beat me," which is almost accurate. It was more like a man detonated when I was too close. I am bothered by "the man I'm living with." What a pale, sad phrase. Not "the man I love." Not even "my boyfriend." Certainly not "my husband."

"I'm totally sorry. Do you want me to call the cops or anything?" He starts to bag my stuff, but he keeps looking at me. He can disguise his curiosity as concern. He can stare at me like a doctor.

"No, that's fine," I say as I push the money towards him.

He pushes the money back. "No, this is on me."

He thinks that, by paying for my Kit Kats and Ho Hos, he is being a white knight in an epic story, that I am lost and wandering.

He does not know that the man who hit me cried about it, that I made it clear that it is over, that I am going home to my parents' comfortable home.

It's only a few minutes later, sitting in the car, that I feel my hands and my eyes unclench. I eat my bagful of crap so fast that I don't remember eating it. It loiters in me. The Ho Hos enter my bloodstream.

I wonder if the man I left in Chicago will be okay. He'd hit me once before but I didn't do anything the first time, because I really thought he was essentially a good guy. Just a guy who doesn't quite know how to play the game. He pursues these arguments that his grad school department disapproves of. He is convinced his papers bear a scrutiny that more correctly aligned students don't receive. Things he worked really hard on were dismissed by the kind of men who are actually bothered by the fact that they haven't won the Nobel Prize. He repeated his rebuttals over and over. He thought that by repeating them often enough to me, he would win with his professors.

When he ranted, he took oxygen from the room. I noticed the cracked linoleum, the yellowed curtains, the thrift store glasses with the tulips on them that now seemed simply trashy. He's evaporated every irony, every jauntiness. He didn't stop; he made the same argument again. I said, to simply restore some air to the room, "Why don't you just assume that your Professor is right. Just for an hour. Just for the hell of it."

His mind spasmed—you can actually see his mind working like an animal behind his eyes—and he hit me. I felt what will become a bruise. I felt blood begin to form between my lips and teeth. I looked at him for a long time, not because I was considering options but because I was on a different planet, and said, "I think this is over." It took three hours to erase the "I think," to expunge the question mark well-behaved girls put in every sentence.

He cried and said, "I'm so sorry. I'm so sorry." We had one of those talks where your sentences get sore. In the end, he begged me not to leave. That was hard. I knew that when I got home, or soon thereafter, there would be another call and this knowledge sat in my throat like a cough.

I couldn't properly wipe my hands and I didn't want to go back into the store. I began the hour drive to Minnisapa with chocolate gunk on my hands.

Something weakened inside me. *He wanted someone to love him. All he wanted was for someone to unconditionally love him.* I started to cry. All he wanted was the power of a woman's love, of which I am evidently incapable. Neither time was the violence the way I imagined it to be. He didn't plan it. He didn't mean it. It was to anger what premature ejaculation is to sex.

And then I remind myself that the asshole hit me. And then the whole argument repeats again.

Is love always an argument? Will I spend my life grunting out forgiveness for some man's weakness, stupidity, self-hate, cluelessness? Does romance always devolve into pity?

I stop at another gas station just north of La Crosse. When I get out of the car, the air is fresher and larger. I yawn. I smell freshly planted fields and maybe some manure. At the end of the parking lot is some ditch grass and then new corn and then some cows. When I realize that the cows had a better night than I had, I get back into the car and cry again. When I compose myself, I wander into the store. It is like an asylum of logos. The Planter's Peanut guy. The Victorian Pringle's guy. The Energizer bunny. And SPAM. Charmin. Tabloids. I wash my hands and face in the bathroom. I look like an alien in the mirror. I get another sympathetic, mute look, this time from a woman behind the counter. I empty the front seat junk into a plastic bag. I wipe the steering wheel off, so it shines.

When I cross the Mississippi and head north, the hills rise up as if the earth were impatient to tell me how beautiful it is. The hills blaze green on my left, the river is on my right. Minnisapa is near. My mom and dad are near.

But when I arrive home, I can hear the phone through the screen door as I climb out of the car onto my sore ankle.

My mother says, "My God, Barb. What happened? Are you okay? He's called three times."

I say, "Everything's okay."

The phone rings twice more.

She says, "Let's just let that go, honey." She's weeping.

I walk toward the phone like one of those zombies in a horror movie. I all but have my arms straight out ahead of me.

Behind me, Mom says, "No, honey. Let it go. He'll call again."

I don't trust myself to be ready a second time. The phone has now rung ten times in my hearing.

I pick it up and press its chaos and plastic to my ear.

"You can't believe how sorry I am."

"Yes, I can. And the strange thing is, it doesn't matter."

"How can you say that?"

"Like this," I say, "*it doesn't matter.*" I hate my glibness here. What an awful, movie-trailer thing to say to someone. But there is a strange pleasure, a craftsmanship, in hurting someone this deftly.

"I'm so sorry. Come back and we can work it out."

"No, we can't."

"Yes, we can."

"You can't say 'we.' You can't say that. Okay? To say 'we' requires my consent."

His angry self comes back. "That's ridiculous. You can't own a fucking pronoun," he lectures.

"This has to be over now. Goodbye."

When I hang up the phone, it is as if he lives in the phone, and I am shutting off his oxygen. I watch the phone for a minute, while he dies. And then I begin to weep, and my mother holds me.

AUTOMOTIVE REPAIR

DEMONSTRATE THE PROPER REPLACEMENT OF BURNED OUT FUSES.

Quint: In the jagged moment, in the staticy air, in the fluorescent light, I take a deep breath; lower my head; lean so far into my cube that it feels as refugelike as a cave, slide open a squeaking metal desk drawer, remove a slip of paper, and read:

> *But the persons I speak of find that all conscious effort leads to nothing but failure and vexation in their hands, and only makes them twofold more the children of hell than they were before. The tense and voluntary attitude becomes in them an impossible fever and torment. Their machinery refuses to run at all when the bearings are made so hot and the belts so tight.*
>
> *Under these circumstances the way to success, as vouched for by innumerable authentic personal narrations, is by an anti-moralistic method, by the 'surrender' of which I spoke in my second lecture. Passivity, not activity; relaxation, not intentness, should be the rule. Give up the feeling of responsibility, let go your hold, resign the care of your destiny to Higher Powers, be genuinely indifferent as to what becomes of it all, and you find that you will gain, not only a perfect inward relief . . .*

The presence—shadow? micro-climate?—of another human

behind me. The unique, muddled sound of someone knocking on whatever the hell it is that covers cube walls.

"Quint. Hey, Quint, let's talk about this in the conference room. The little one by the copier."

I turn. "Yeah. Sure. Just give me a sec."

Surrender. Relaxation. Resignation. I'm not quite there yet, but this is close enough. An abrasiveness recedes, just enough, for now.

HIKING

Chimes: Ever been the last guy at a party? After Slocum moved up to the Cities, I realized that I was the last of our high-school crowd to live in Minnisapa.

The thing is, I'm a celebrity, albeit the single most low-watt celebrity in the history of the world. I can't go into the Go-Mart to buy a fruit cup without some doof announcing, "Hey, Keith." Or, worse yet, "Hey, it's the bowling-alley guy." The people who know me call me "Chimes." Nobody calls me Chimes anymore.

This isn't what I thought I would wind up doing, even though I've always loved bowling. Bowling got me in the papers, when I bowled a three-hundred game. After that 270 on the ninth frame, I got so nervous I had to take a crap. There is a certain kind of bowel movement that is about as close as I ever get to prayer. You lean forward and clasp your hands and clench until you finally calm the hell down. My prayers to Saint Brunswick, patron saint of bowling, must have been answered. Because I went out there and nailed it. I knew that I'd nailed it the moment the ball left my hand. I shattered the fuckers. They somersaulted; they leapt to their death.

I thought I'd be a sitcom writer and work in some office in

a city. I saw myself exchanging witticisms with the receptionist when I strolled-in in the morning—you know us writers, we can't be expected to be punctual—like in the *Dick Van Dyke Show*. I figured I'd come up with the kind of stuff that *TV Guide* would later immortalize with phrases like "madcap antics" and "hilarious consequences ensue." Then, I'd come home and Mary Tyler Moore would be waiting for me in Capri pants.

Instead, I'm working the Tuesday night shift and a three-hundred-pound woman in stretch pants from the Ladies League comes up to me and orders "a bag of Funyuns and a Fresh-ca." I can barely restrain myself from yelling, "It's Fres-ca, you stupid bitch. There's no 'h' in it." And then she introduces me to some hillbilly cousin of hers: "This is my good friend Keith. He's the bowling-alley guy."

I don't know. People have real problems. I should be grateful. I've got a little house, albeit a rented one next to a bar and the railroad tracks. I've got a job that doesn't totally suck. A couple of months ago, I even got laid, but it was just one of those drunk things, a single mom who gets away from her kid once a month and fucks somebody. The next time you see her, she's with her ex.

Maybe that's why it felt so good when Barb Carimona moved back. She'd been shacking up with some guy who was studying for a Ph.d. in Chicago. And then the next thing we knew she was back in Minnisapa, working the counter at the GoMart at Bunke and Schuth.

You see, Barb's from the old crowd, the people who would hang out together in the concourse in high school and make smart remarks to the edification of passers-by. She's one of the people who would gather at the Quarry that one great summer when we were all nineteen and people were all still in town. We would spend whole afternoons out on the beach and all sorts of different people would show up. The sun on the water and the leaves that would shimmer in the breeze and the sixteen-ounce Budweisers and buckets of Kentucky Fried Chicken were about as good as it gets. There was a lot of banter. Banter is underrated.

So that's why it was so cool when I walked into the convenience store where Barb works now and she said to me, "Chimes, I've been thinking about the essence of Chuck Nuscent."

Nuscent was our homecoming king and, while not a bad guy, was a little too pleased with himself.

She looks at me, waits for an imaginary drum roll, and says, "Every male lead on the Love Boat." And she's right. And she leans back on the cashier's stool, proud, her eyes twinkling a little.

Quint King, who actually thinks about shit like this, says that when you notice that a woman has pretty eyes, that what you're doing is acknowledging that she's a spiritual being. The problem is, I have yet to recognize that I'm a spiritual being.

I recently took up hiking. Go figure.

I'd wake up on a Saturday morning, a little hungover, and in no mood to deal with the mess in my house. My plan was to drive to the woods by the hills on the edge of town where Smash and Slow and I would hike as kids, when we weren't down by the river putting frogs out of their misery. Sometimes you just get a hankering for dead twigs and moldy leaves and the other glories of nature.

But I needed fuel, not having bothered to make myself breakfast. I stopped at the convenience store where Barb worked.

She said, "You gonna watch the movie about Minnisapa

tonight?"

Some lame-ass mystery novel by some Minnisapa State prof had been made into a movie-of-the-week.

"Wouldn't miss it," I said.

"I'm sure it will live up to the *high standards for realism* we've come to expect from TV movies," she said. Her eyes twinkle a little.

I bought some donuts of the month. The Minnisapa convenience mart has a donut of the month that they name after some local character. It's considered an honor. I'm not sure anybody has really thought it through. You are eventually going to run out of people who might plausibly inspire a donut design. This month's donuts were orange and black, the school colors in honor of the football coach, a decent enough guy who taught me geography or something. The black frosting was licorice. Six of those babies and a coffee the size of a bulk tank and I'm good to go. I figure I can piss in the woods.

Barb pulls her hands of out the pouch of her sweatshirt. She says, "And yet you maintain your boyish figure."

Boyish figure, indeed.

I decided to put those donuts to good use and actually climb the fucking hill and not just meander around the lower woods like a country gentleman. I had my eye on this outcropping that I hadn't stood on in fifteen years. It was hard to get to, but when you stood there, it was like a balcony overlooking the whole town.

The ground was muddy. Trees that—let's just say—are elms. Rocks with lichen or something else that lost the evolution lottery. I started sucking wind about halfway up. It felt like it might rain. I kept slipping and getting mud on my knees. Fucking raspberry bushes. Last year's leaves and old hunks of trees and twigs everywhere. I'd put on some of those yellow farmer gloves. I was glad I did. They were covered with mud and full of burrs and crap by the time I was halfway up.

When I got to the ledge, I could see birds flying below me. My hangover got the best of me; it swirled in my head, and I stepped back from the ledge. I could see the crappy green bluffs across the river in Wisconsin and the crappy brown river and the dome of Saint Mark's church. The town itself looked exactly like a broken wing. You could tell that Lake Minnisapa had been a part of the river until some goofball flipped a barge. I could see the high school. The hospital. And out of the corner of my eye, the bowling alley, and under some trees, my parents' house and my house.

The traffic on Highway 61 looked like a video game. So this is it? I thought. This is my life? I felt dizzy and my head hurt but I wasn't sorry I came up here.

I thought of how I would describe this to Barb at the convenience store. "I felt like Mussolini on the balcony." I like that. Nicely phrased. Barb is the only person I'm going to talk to in the foreseeable future who will get the reference. You have to love my customers but they think Mussolini is the little mouse on *Ed Sullivan*.

And then I had one of those moments that you don't know what the hell to make of. It was like repeating a word over and over again until it becomes strange. You know, say "pretzels" twenty times and it messes with your head. It was one of those moments when you realize, and I know that this sounds nuts, that you are only you, and you are all you will ever be, and that you are going to die. And the next thing you know you're looking at the little hairs on your knuckles and they look like nothing you've ever seen before. The next thing you know you're about four minutes from joining the seminary.

Maybe it was my light head, but the way Marcotte Street

ran across the lake and through town and then over the river to Wisconsin or the way I could recognize the rectangle of streets that had formed our neighborhood when we were kids and the way Munson Avenue followed the lake seemed the most beautiful thing in the world. Every street made me remember everything I'd done for three decades, give or take: Walking home from school up Bunke Street, or playing touch football by Quint's or walking home from Monopoly tournaments at Pooch's, or hanging around with Smash on the railroad tracks.

Then I shifted my weight and accidentally kicked a rock over the ledge and scared the hell out of myself. That rock took its time hitting the ground and stopping rolling.

I got the hell out of there. I felt like I was in God's chair and he wanted it back.

I went home and cleaned my house for the first time in months and took a bath. My muscles hurt.

I flipped on the Sunday night movie, and it was the usual crap, until I realized that it was the one based on a mystery written by a Minnisapa State professor, of all things. They even set it in Minnisapa. This is the only time in my entire life that Minnisapa has ever been mentioned for any reason in the national media. Except for that one time Jimmy Carter took a riverboat trip and all the Jaycees stood on the levee in their yellow blazers and waved at him.

Of course, the clowns who made the movie got it all wrong. One couple said to the other: "We have you guys for dinner on Saturday?" No one in the history of Minnisapa has ever said that, I thought. The old gang would have riffed on that for weeks. We would have met each other in the high school hallway, a bunch of skinny-ass kids in tennis shoes and Steely Dan T-shirts saying:

"Did you get the trig assignment?" "Yeah. And we've got you guys for dinner on Saturday?" We knew how to milk a joke.

I didn't bother to watch the movie. I just kept it on when I was in the tub. For some reason, TV is louder and weirder when you are in the tub. It bounces around on the wall and you can't turn the damn thing down.

"We've got you guys for dinner?"

Please.

I had to talk to somebody about how stupid this was but there was nobody to tell about it. Pooch was out in the Northwest somewhere and Slow was in the Cities, and who knows where Smash was. Of course, Barb was around. I decided to tell her about it the next day. I thought of calling her; I think she's living with her parents, but I'm not really a phone guy. You miss the full panorama that is me.

The next day, I'm so eager to get to work, I get up before noon.

I make my regular visit to the convenience store. I'm not awake yet. My thoughts consist of a vague contempt for my fellowman.

Barb says, "Check out the new donut of the month." And there they are, in with the long johns and éclairs and crullers: big glazed donuts with x's marked on them with chocolate. The card, in Barb's loopy handwriting, says: "November's Donut of the Month. The Keith 'Chimes' Sanborn."

The x's represent strikes. A bowling motif.

I feel like I already had about a dozen donuts and a gallon of coffee and am starting to vibrate. Barb is saying, "Yeah, Mr. Manager and I thought it was cool that, when you bought a dozen, you got a three-hundred game."

I feel like I just bowled a three hundred game.

I am standing on a ledge, looking over the town, from two hundred feet up. I am above the birds. I am a word repeated a million times.

SKATING

Quint: There can be a moment when the world is allowed to be what it is. There can be a moment when the static of irritation is silenced and when the nausea of fear is calmed and when one's connection to one's fellow humans is warmly assumed and when the world feels like enough and when enough feels like more than enough. There can be a moment when the idea of death is not a personal gravity in your head and heart and hands. There can be a moment when even though the human voice has been encrusted with the usual crap—agendas, delusions, banality, grievance, naval-gazing, clichés, Hallmarkisms, and the eternal struggle to get the pretty girls to notice us—the voices of others can still deliver the incandescence of the human soul.

At such a lucky pivot, you hear a wobble in a voice that suggests sincerity, a statement against self-interest that suggests "this is not bullshit," a detail that says, "I am not just repeating something but giving you a true report of what is inside of me." There is a moment when you have held hands and prayed with people—some of them strangers, some not—and the aura of this stays with you. You emerge from a beige room that smells like cigarettes and coffee. You pass through a screen door, and hunch your shoulders at the April chill and nod at a gaggle of quasi-hipster smokers who nod back at you with a nod that actually seems to say, "*dude*," and then, when you descend the three steps to the walkway, you feel a certain lightness, you feel this *bounce* which is a cousin to the feeling you felt while playing outside as a kid and you light up a cigarette of your own and feel its warm gritty sense of resolution swirl into your lungs and you appreciate the way it gives your hands deft little tasks and gestures as you begin to walk to the apartment you rent in a run-down house in a nice enough neighborhood. There are times when consciousness is not a flickering polluted strident arctic thing but the stuff that warms the stuff of the universe. There are times when the April weather—look: a bird balancing on a rain-slicked wire and apparently swearing at himself—seems glorious. There are times when, as you cross a side street, you notice one of those weirdly complicated plastic lids for milkshakes with like eight cross hairs and complicated coding for various milkshake contingencies. The milkshake lid drifts with the damp April wind into one of those plants with the leaves that are green and wet and the complex little white flowers that look like clusters of asterisks. There are times when the snaggle-toothed guy who works on the apartments around here sees you and smiles and says "hello" while he is walking a happy dog and lets you pet the dog who is not just wiggling and tail-twitching but sort of bobbing and weaving and almost genuflecting with the sheer joy of encountering another being. You know this will not last: Something annoying will happen, or this feeling will subtly degrade, but you don't think about that now. For now, the world is a happy dog squirming under your hand.

FAMILY LIFE

PREPARE AND OUTLINE WITH YOUR MERIT BADGE COUNSELOR WHAT A FAMILY IS AND HOW THE ACTIONS OF ONE MEMBER CAN AFFECT OTHER MEMBERS.

Barb: I'm totally in take-care-of-myself mode when it happens. I'm waking up every morning and spooning out freeze-dried crystals and drinking my sudsy coffee beneath the halo of a fluorescent light, while my mom and dad sleep in the next room. I'm walking to work every day. I'm breathing the fresh air. I'm applying the dawn like a compress on my psychic bruises. (I laid low until the real ones went away.) I'm walking past the houses I've known since I was a girl. That's where the Kings used to stare out at the street, waiting for the plow to pass on snow days, as if they were an audience for a parade no one else knew about; that's where the two old-maid sisters would yell, "Hi, honey, we're praying for you"; down that street is where the guys played touch football. I'm walking past these houses as if they knew everything I once knew about moderation and decency. I'm walking past these houses as if they welcomed me, as if they did not think I'm a failure. Walking this walk is like saying a rosary.

When I get to the Go Mart, I make the coffee and set out the food to be warmed in the rotisserie and update the signage. Then I install myself behind the counter and ring up people's purchases of gas and breath mints and beef jerky. Sometimes Chimes Sanborn stops by on his way to work.

I've done all that stuff for the tenth morning in a row and I'm feeling totally blissed out on routine. I'm feeling blissed out on working at the Go Mart when I hear the honking. There are two customers at the counter and we all look to see what's going on. Someone comes toward the store with a concerned look on her face. A middle-aged lady. She disturbs the reflections on the door when she comes in. She says, "There's a child on the road."

"What?"

"There's a child. Wandering. All by herself. A little girl."

We rush out, and there the girl is. She's maybe three. All she's wearing is her panties. She's chubby.

There are ten cars backed up behind her. It's as if she's woken up in the intersection. She falls down and starts to suck her thumb.

My stomach lightens and I run. I pick her up. "It's okay, honey," I say.

"Are you sure we shouldn't wait for the police to arrive," the woman says.

"She's not a bomb," I say. And then I say into the top of the little girl's head, "Everything's okay." She's heavier than I expected and warm, but she doesn't smell good. She squirms beneath my chin but doesn't say anything. Her flesh is rubbery and cold against my arms.

I bring her in the store and go behind the counter and set her down. Two policeman arrive before I can pick up the phone.

I say, "Honey, these men are going to take care of you."

The little girl sucks harder on her thumb. Her eyes are so empty and sad they might as well be the sky. She starts to shake.

I act on a hunch.

I say, "Sir, I think she might need to use the bathroom. And could you come with me, given what's happened."

He nods and does. I carry her into the bathroom. She's silent but still shaking. I almost drop her and she slides down my legs. I hunker down and say, "Honey, I'm going to put you on the toilet now." I slide her panties down and that's when I see the cigarette burns.

I don't really remember the rest of the day. Everything glowed: The yellow and red snouts of the gas additives. The green spiral notebooks. It's like what it must feel like to come back from the dead. It's totally sad and totally happy at the same time. I thought: we have such a lame sense of what constitutes a miracle. Everything is a damn miracle.

But it was icky, too. Every color seemed richer because a three-year-old girl was tortured by her stepfather. Her pain was a color swatch that I held up against my life, to better see my happiness.

Still, they tell me I saved her. They tell me she will be okay.

SNOW SPORTS

DEMONSTRATE YOUR ABILIITY . . . TO COPE WITH AN AVERAGE VARIETY OF SNOW CONDITIONS.

Quint: Sober four years, and stuff still comes out. Like those Vietnam vets who wake up and see a piece of shrapnel sneaking out of their forearms like a rat. For twenty years, I have not had emotions about my father so much as I've had these kind of *anti-emotions* and for decades these things have ricocheted around within my numb, dumb soul in ways that I could only vaguely sense. They're like those imaginary numbers that you have to be a physicist or Pooch Labrador to even *suspect*. Or like ghosts, which are more my speed. I do know that something nudged me my whole life toward the usual cocktail of self-destruction and self-loathing and self-sabotage and the usual unlivable combination of numbness and rawness, arrogance and bafflement. But it is only now, on a Christmas morning, in this beautiful house in Saint Paul that my girlfriend and I have rented and where we are hiding away on Christmas, that I recognized this. It has snowed and the snow is like love and loneliness at the same time. Shoveling it seems sacrilege, so I move slowly when I push it from the sidewalks and jab it away from the steps, but still the shovel makes those scraping sounds and those ugly signatures. But the yard is perfect and it is not until after that, when I have taken off my boots and smacked them to get rid of the snow that dusts them, when I have been amazed once more at this beautiful woman in the kitchen and this big green great-smelling *tree* in my living room, all tarted up with ornaments and all goofy with presents; it is only when I have had my manly cocoa with the little undissolved pimples of powder; and it is only when I have ascended to the big bathroom with the skylight and have gotten into the shower and I can see more snow tumbling and sliding down the skylight like kids down a hill and the mist is rising and steaming up everything in sight and maybe, for once, unclogging that weird little thing in my ear and when I have begun to think about all these stupid boyhood presents—like an obnoxious one-man band with a rubber-nosed horn and the hopeless optimism of a Twister game and plastic pinball games that break in like three days—that something suddenly comes over me and I realize how much I miss my father and that I have missed him for twenty years and I begin to sob.

AMERICAN CULTURES

IMAGINE THAT ONE OF THE GROUPS (OF
AMERICANS YOU'VE CHOSEN TO STUDY) HAD
ALWAYS LIVED ALONE IN A CITY OR COUNTRY TO
WHICH NO OTHER GROUPS EVER CAME.

Slow: I have a job designing mailboxes, a great wife, and three kids who are too young to have gone dope fiend on me. We recently moved from a three-bedroom house on one cul-de-sac to a four-bedroom house on a nearby cul-de-sac. You would think that would be cool. But it was a profoundly dube experience.

For some reason, moving freaked everybody out. Most of it was just the usual weird stuff about moving: The way that packing tape screams when you rip it from the tape dispenser thing; the walls with the stigmata where the pictures used to hang; the dust-and-sock prairie where the bed used to be.

But then Patricia is packing up our five-year-old's room, and I hear these yells.

"No, Mommy! No!"

"What, Jennifer? Why do you want to keep this?"

"Because I want to."

"But we need to throw out the things that aren't important. And these are just silly."

"No! No! NO!"

"NO. NEVER HIT MOMMY!"

I'm in the room by now. Our eleven-year-old tries to sneak in with me and I redirect him into the living room. Patricia is holding two pictures ripped out of magazines. One is of former Canadian Prime Minister Brian Mulroney frying fish at some campground; the other is a *TV Guide* ad with this bad-attitude lizard who is a spokeslizard for Budweiser. Both pictures are both ripped so three sides are straight and one is coastline-shaped.

Jennifer has calmed down and isn't punching her mom.

"Why do you want to keep these, honey?"

She doesn't want to answer and starts to cry.

I drop to a squat so I look at her face to face, so I don't look like so much of a dad.

"Are these special to you for some reason?"

"Yes. They're my friends."

My eleven-year-old has snuck back in the room. "Man, you're a freak."

"Shut up," Jennifer screams at her brother.

"Freakazoid. Freak! Freak! Freakazoid!"

"You're not helping, Sam. Leave."

I try to remember being a kid. When I was little, I imagined some weird stuff. "Do you make up adventures with them?"

She shakes her head yes.

I wonder if she'll make lists. I wonder if she'll make semi-secret lists of things she thinks are cool and if she'll consult them when she's sad.

I look up at Patricia. She tells me to go ahead.

I say to Jennifer, "Because you hit your mommy, I'm going to keep them in my office for a month, and then I'll give them back to you."

She looks at me and says, "Okay." But then she starts to cry, because she will miss the lizard and the prime minister of our Good Neighbor to the North. The baby starts to scream in a way that suggests that Sam provoked it. When we get there and see that there's no crisis, just Sam hovering with the tape dispenser, Patricia whispers to me, "You punished her by grounding her imaginary friends?" We look at each other with a look that says we're both too busy to fight.

I joke about the configuration of frozen yogurt franchises, drive up banks, and Pizza Huts that I call home, but I'm comfortable here. I love the frontage roads and the white "left turn" and "go straight" arrows on the lanes and the green freeway signs, and the strips of grass and trees by, say, a mall, and the low new industrial buildings with reflective, coffee-colored walls of windows and the brand new health club looking out over cornfields. The health club has a spire like a church, which I sometimes think is blasphemous and sometimes think is cool. Because I design mailboxes in an office park five minutes from our home (either the new or the old home), I rarely get out of our suburb.

But, still, you get to know a lot about the world designing mailboxes in an industrial park. People will steal from mailboxes, will attack them, will spill food in them because they can't bother to finish their chili dog before they check the slot. We hold focus groups with mail carriers, and you just can't believe the stuff that happens to mailboxes. You design them so you can wash off blood and other bodily fluids. Washing off blood shouldn't be a design criteria. Not in a civilized society.

There's always some dube pushing the depravity envelope, pushing the stupidity envelope. We have what we call idiot sessions where we think of the stupidest possible things you could do to a mailbox, and they're never good enough; some real idiot always comes up with something we haven't thought of. We try to design it so you can lick it and then bite it. Then we pretend that we're a four-year-old who thinks it would make a great medieval knight's head, and we design for *that* and then someone will completely fool us by flossing with it. "I just had something stuck in my teeth and I tried to use your mailbox to get dislodge it and look what happened. I'm suing."

Even Minnisapa had its bad element. The guys I hung around with would make fun of the hoods, who skipped school and smoked dope. Guys like Scott Tulep, who wouldn't eat the regular lunch during j-high but would instead buy ice cream sandwiches from this little concession stand in the lunchroom and stand around and harass people. They'd mooch fries, hovering over some cowering kid and saying, "Hey, can I borrow a fry?" In high school, I'd call up my friend Pooch and say, "Hey, your buddy Scott Tulep called and said you were supposed to pick up the beer and the smokes. He said he was gonna kick your ass." By that time, I don't think we even saw Tulep and those guys around anymore. They must have dropped out. I never even thought about what the rest of their lives must be like.

On the weekend we actually moved, Patricia took the kids down to Grandma's in Minnisapa, and I stayed around, with just a sleeping bag and a toilet kit and a cell phone for ordering pizza. Getting ready for that night, I'd had my one little consumerist thrill: As a treat, I bought my toiletries in travel sizes, because I used to think they looked so cool sitting in my dad's toilet kit when I was a kid. Patricia thinks my obsession with travel-kit toiletries is a little weird. But besides that, I'm a straight I'll-have-what-he's-having guy. I prefer brand names because, to me, that just means that somebody knows what they're doing, somebody's got that taken care of, so I can throw it in the cart and focus on my family and my job and my relationship with God. I don't have to spend half my life searching for the perfect latte-flavored shampoo.

I was feeling a little hincty because Patricia and I had a fight before she left, ostensibly because she thought Sam was old enough to help, and I, on the other hand, didn't want him in the way, but really because we'd both worked all week and then packed all night, because the barely contained chaos of family life wasn't really contained anymore, because we had actually literally made ourselves homeless, although I know a real homeless guy who stumbled into our house, even with just the bare walls and everything packed up, would think he was staying at the Ritz.

It was weird being alone, without my wife and kids, with even the stupid cats in a kennel, with no TV, with just me sleeping on the carpet of the living room, in my slippery mummy-shaped sleeping bag, the curtains all packed away, the windows bare, moonlight flooding into the house, and the shadows changing the boxes into Stongehenges. I hadn't been that alone in years.

The next morning, the movers showed up half-an-hour late, which didn't seem to bother them.

"Well, we've got a lot to do, so let's get started and make up some time," I said, because I didn't want to start off by yelling at them, but I wanted to impress a little urgency on them. Half the people who show up at your house to do something don't have any sense of urgency whatsoever. Sometimes I don't think they've ever heard of a market economy.

"We can only move so fast," said a tall guy with a kind of seventies haircut and a porn star attitude. "And Junior here is pretty hung over and needs his smoke breaks."

"Shut up," Junior said. Junior was pumped up with weights and tattooed as a comic book. He had one of those droopy mustaches that looked like an auxiliary smirk. Then, to my surprise, these guys started to move pretty fast. They let me help. (Otherwise I would just stand around like a dube.) And we had this brisk line going and we'd nod as we passed with boxes or returned to the house in that we're-guys-doing-a-job kind of way.

And then something else happened: I dropped a vase, which shattered on the kitchen floor. I realized that I knew Junior. Or at least I think I did, because of a way he squinted his mouth and pushed down his long chin, like he was concentrating the nastiness in whatever he had to say. He said, "you broke it, you bought it," and laughed at me.

His face and his story came into my head.

One night, when I was in Minnisapa for Christmas, when people were still hanging around at the holidays, some guys robbed a local jewelry store wearing weird masks, like Nixon masks but of some other guy. Because no one could see the robber's faces, the news reports were hilarious and pure Minnisapa. "Two white males in their early twenties, between 5'10" and 6' are suspected in the robbery." And, because that described 60% of the guys we knew, my friends and I kept threatening to turn each other in.

The video of the robbery wasn't funny, though. They'd used guns and terrified the cashiers as men in those weird masks can terrify people; they'd made people start crying and begging for their life, and they'd flashed guns and barked commands and hauled off jewelry. The masks made it worse, made it horrible, made everything feel like what rape must feel like. They weren't some poor schmoes who needed the cash and shook while they held the guns. They wanted to mess you up so that you could never be cleaned up again. The robbery was almost an afterthought. They just wanted to put the biggest dose of horrible in your head that they could.

About a year later somebody realizes that the mask was a mask of Canadian Prime Minister Brian Mulroney, and then later somebody learned that Scott Tulep had worked on oil rigs in Canada. And he had come home to visit his uncle that Christmas but had never come back since. Junior the Mover, I now realized, was Scott Tulep.

And so I stood there and worked with this guy and made small talk with him as he carried boxes marked with the names of my children and my wife and placed them in the home where my family would live. I tried to watch him as he looked around my house, in that appraising way that movers do, and as he made small talk about the place, and grinned his oily winking grin, and made an expression like he was sucking on a lemon, but all the clues were too subtle, and, after a while, I think he knew that I knew who he was, and that made him smirk even more.

So I asked, "You guys from around here?"

And the boss guy said, "Do we look like we're from around here?" He meant that they didn't look like they were from our suburb, which the Twin Cities TV stations always call "fashionable."

"I mean Minnesota. The upper Midwest."

Junior said, "I'm from Nowhere."

I tried to joke, "That's funny. So am I."

"It's a big fuckin' town," he said, and winked at me.

It's been a month now and nothing has happened, but sometimes I still have trouble sleeping and wait and watch, sitting on our couch at two in the morning, looking at the black of the picture window, the driveway, the military cut lawn and the neighbors' houses and driveways and lawns and cars in the darkness. I stare like a soldier in a jungle. I am thousands of miles away from home.

FORESTRY

PREPARE . . . A WRITTEN DESCRIPTION OF . . . THE FOREST'S SUCCESSIONAL STAGE, WHAT ITS HISTORY HAS BEEN, AND WHAT ITS FUTURE IS.

Quint: How was I spending the clarity that was the gift of eight years of sobriety? I was free-associating in the closety, humming air of a plane twenty-thousand feet above Whoknowswhere. I was thinking about the Mad Moose brand, whose tagline is "Proactively Stupid" and whose signature products are a peanut butter white-chocolate cereal, a banana almond-bark cereal, and an orange-chocolate cereal that they market as a hangover remedy. I was thinking, *on some level a bagel is a natural extension of a cereal* because a bagel is just a gigantic toasty o; and I was thinking that they would succeed because all previous bagel makers tried to start with authentic bagels and Midwestern them down but that Mad Moose should not even try to be authentic; they should take the Las Vegas-in-a-bowl breakfast cereal ethos and just slap it onto bagels. And I was firing up my laptop, waiting for its airy whir and blinking awakening. My eyes dried a little; my shoulders hunched a little; I heard the chipmunky sounds of my fingers key-entering my thoughts. And that is what I was doing, as best I can recreate it, at the exact time that a stroke fizzed through my mother's brain and she collapsed, alone in her house in Minnisapa, to lie on the floor for twenty hours in a chaos of Hummel figurines. Some of the figurines had cut her.

Who forgets the glowing triviality and intramural pettiness of the moments before you hear bad news? A day off the plane, I sat in a conference room and brainstormed with my clients about potential brand extensions. Me, my friend the CEO, a new executive who seemed to be a numbers guy, a brand manager, a graphic designer, and a project manager. It was one of those brainstorms where your brain actually surged and sparked, where ideas lurked in coffee cups the way motion lurks in oil; where thoughts flew against whiteboards as if of their own momentum. People looked in the same direction, people leaned forward with energy or leaned back with ease, people smiled at each other with asides. The pretty young project manager wrote the ideas on the white paper as if she were pleased that they passed through her hand. *Bagels in refillable day glo disks, the Why-not-reinvent-the-Wheel? sweepstakes, bagel sundaes, advertising budgets shifted from more traditional media to 5,000 painted hubcaps, bagels placed in rent-a-cars, "I can't believe-it's not-a-donut!"* My buddy got up, made a mock-humble CEO joke about how the ideas will improve as soon as he leaves, and smacked my shoulder. *Crackerjack prizes, cartoony illustrated panels like on old cereal boxes, edible yo yos.*

The new executive had been quiet. It turned out that he was from one of the more traditional food companies and that he was kind of a dick. He said, "We've had our fun. Now, which of these are we going to focus group?"

If you can't be creative, I guess you can infantilize the people who are.

"That's not really the style here," I said. "Focus groups don't test concepts; they test group dynamics." Some flare of disgust hardened my words. And when I said, "That's not really the style here," I'd implied that I knew more about his company than he did. Of course, I did.

"But you make a great point," I said. "The next step is to sort out winners." Was this enough to placate him? Was "great point" sucking up too much? As he was looking at me, he looked down and his irritation focused into contempt. I looked down, saw a glistening little plastic thorax, and realized that I'd been chewing on my pen cap, and it had fallen off; it was all bent, wet and indented with bite marks, revealing the chipmunk within the consultant, something nervous and spitty within me. I quickly picked it up and reattached it.

"I'm working for you guys. I can write up the notes," I said. I might as well have just rolled on my back and showed him my nuts. At that point, an executive assistant entered the room as tactfully as a draft and said there was a phone call for me. I turn my cell phone off when I'm with a client, so at first I was annoyed that someone was being so pushy. Then, as I left the conference room, the other possibilities for such a call occurred to me. Putting the phone to my ear felt like stepping to the edge of a cliff.

I needed to move to catch a plane home that night, a half day before I'd intended. Of my siblings, I was the one to rush home. As I put my cell phone to my ear, and heard the pigeony insistence of it ringing my home, I looked through the vent in the shield that separated me from my cabbie. He'd posted a large picture of what must be his daughter above his dash. When my wife picked up, I pressed the cell phone closer to my face and let her know that I was coming home early. I didn't need to tell her much; she heard from the hospital before I did.

Freeway sound-dampening walls and other traffic and airport buildings flowed past. The picture of the cabby's daughter, my wife's voice, this cloudy barrier: I wanted to hug my son or touch my wife. For the past forty-eight hours, I'd touched what lonely single men touch: phones and keys, keyboards and remotes and pens, hands offered in handshakes, glasses sanitized for my protection, room service lids, my dick. I slapped payment and 20% tip into the cabby's hand, grabbed my luggage, and piloted its annoying needy mass, on rollers, behind me through the automatic doors. I walked briskly among brisk strangers.

Once I cleared security, I started to worry. If I'd stayed another half day, I'd have seen the CEO again. We were buddies; I'd practically founded the company with him. I'd have seen the financial executive again and I could have diluted the bad first impression I'd made, but that wasn't to be. Mom was tugging me home. I resented her, and felt like a chump for doing so. On the plane, I looked out the plastic window at the night and looked forward at the grey and orange pattern of the seat back. I opened my laptop, but then remembered the notes were on big flopping sheets of paper. For lack of anything better to do, I prayed: the serenity prayer, half-phrases from books I don't read enough: "free me from the bondage of self." My prayers skimmed and failed to calm me. I thought instead of the lap pool I'd built in my backyard, my gift to myself when my consulting business had a great year. I saw myself tonight when I got home or tomorrow, before leaving, in my swim trunks, immersing myself in turquoise, illuminated water, its gallons slipping past me as I swam and as I turned to gasp air that was not the air of a conference room or a cab or a plane. But then I realized that, if I were to take a swim, I would lose an hour I couldn't lose.

It was almost eleven when I drove my car away from the parking ramp, and I exited past the grass and native rock knoll that welcomes me to Saint Paul. The Mississippi flowed beneath me. Darkened parks lined the river. I insist on living here, because the first time I drove down Cretin Avenue, it reminded me of Minnisapa, even though I appeared to have been alone among my classmates in winding up in Saint Paul. About a month ago, I'd run into Slow Slocum at an oriental buffet in one of the western suburbs. I'd been wary of Slow ever since I heard him refer to me as a dope fiend in high school, but I'd run into him every so often and realized that he's just a guy trying to keep it together and that he worships at the church of whatever makes you less crazy. He told me that Barb Carimona wound up here after a bad boyfriend in Chicago and some time laying low in Minnisapa and Slow even maintained that Scott Tulep had moved him into his McMansion. We talked about Smash, who I imagined behind the wheel, burning across the country. But Slow thought he was back in Minnisapa. Chimes, at the bowling alley, would know.

When he mentioned that Barb had wound up here–via law school, law practice, family on a cul de sac–I thought about Sarah, who I'd lost touch with after she broke up with me. Slow had heard that she was the head of some non-profit in the Pacific Northwest. When I thought of my cultural contribution—a trademarked moose—and my great psychological insight—bagel as stealth donut—*Annie Hall* felt like a promise I'd broken. When I left that lunch, I got my self-centered, over-sensitive ass to a room where a bunch of recovering drunks sat around the table and a bunch of clichés hectored me from the wall; I unburdened myself to strangers and I prayed to a higher vagueness and felt better.

There is nothing more beautiful than a house with a light left on for you. Still compressed and stale from the plane, I walked in the entry way, and hugged Carol as she emerged from her office. I held her longer than normal, felt her shoulders, and touched her hair.

It turned out that her call from the hospital had been stranger than mine.

"When the nurse called, we talked a little. It seems your mom's been kind of freaked out. She said, 'Satan' a couple of times. They think she may have thought she was being possessed."

"Jesus," I said.

Carol's face tipped me off to the irony of what I'd just said. She paused long enough for us both to realize that there wasn't much more to say about that, and then she said, "I know this is an awful time. But there are two checks you need to write out tonight." I'd forgotten to write them out before I'd left on this trip. I suddenly felt how exhausted I was and how much I wanted to see Clyde, our son.

"Can I do it before I leave tomorrow? I promise. I'm just so tired."

She didn't say anything, because we both knew I was asking her to pretty much disown what she just said. My mom's stroke gave me a little pass.

I said, "I think I'm going to look in on Clyde."

"You woke it, you bought it," she said. It's a household joke.

He didn't even stir; he'd simplified to his breathing. I quickly and quietly shut the door.

Anxious, I got up early. I prayed to make the nausea of fear in my gut go away. I signed the two checks. I cringed at the mess in my office, I cringed at my cluelessness about our bank balance, I cringed because the car needed to be taken in, I cringed because I needed to be taken in (for my bleeding gums, my crunching back, my itching forehead), I cringed because my son appeared to be heading off for college. I cringed at my unfiled email; I cringed because I'd never quite gotten around to syncing my home and office computer and that now computers are just one more thing to let get messy; I cringed because I should send invoices. I cringed because here I was trying to make the world safe for the imperial ambitions of breakfast cereal and entropy appeared to be outflanking me. I was making myself late; I procrastinated in ways so subtle they were almost mystical. I deleted some emails; moved some files into folders; wrote down my client's number. I then sat in my chair and prayed, but it felt like procrastination. When I prayed, I pressed my fingertip into my cheek and chewed on it like an eight-year-old.

I slipped out of Saint Paul along the river, on Warner Road, which only the locals know. It glides under bridges and past bike paths and bovine barges and the jostling water; when it clears downtown on the left, it passes wooded hills which are normally charismatic with caves. This all normally soothes me, but this morning I felt like I was all exposed guts, like the world was a fan I wanted to turn off. A pressure that wasn't quite tears welled behind my eyes. I turned onto Highway 61 and I headed south through this unsacramental damn landscape, past the railroad yards and the thick trees and then past the twiggy suburban developments and taco and burger places and the gas station signs on four story stalks.

The highway unspooled in my dirty windshield; one of the lesser ELO songs played on the radio; the fear in my gut became a picture in my mind: me, alone, confused as if in a dream, arthritic, in a house, all alone, leaving the world, everyone I love somewhere else. Where are my wife and son? Dead, distant, estranged, not here.

About halfway down to Minnisapa, I pulled into a fast food place drive-up and ordered a breakfast sandwich and coffee, which a pleasant woman about my mom's age handed to me. I chomped through its buttery strata and swallowed it in the parking lot, because I'll get it all over myself otherwise. I tossed the greasy metallic blossom of its wrapper onto the floor of my car. I felt a weird, doglike embarrassment sitting here. My coffee won't cool until Minnisapa. I thought to blow on it, but let it alone. I thought to empty the car of its accumulated trash, but didn't. My mother was alone, lost in her staticy and satanic mind. But I did make one call, to my Mad Moose client. I left a voice mail for the financial executive.

"Hi, Quint King here, I'm getting everything typed up this morning and sent to you." I wished I'd said "today" rather than "this morning."

I pulled onto the highway and accelerated.

Minnisapa had oozed northward. A kind of truck city—SuperAmerica, a motel, a diner, fuel tanks like dinosaur eggs, dozens of detached cabs on gravel lots—had appeared in what used to be fields, just north of the Pits where Sarah and Chimes and Smash and, well, everyone and I sunned and swam that summer before I went into the Navy. And, then, I saw cut trees and piled dirt and Tyvek and equipment and the beginnings of foundations on the shore of what used to be the Quarry. A sign said Site of Premier TownHomes and gave a phone number. The last time I returned, I discovered that Papa Tony's was an Applebees—the red and white oilcloths, the little napkin dispensers, all erased—and before that that the Regal Theater was a beauty supplies distributorship: the smell of popcorn, the particular softness of movie seats, the foresty charm of a dark movie theater, the memory of Smash throwing an apple core through the screen, Annie Hall in her vest and tie and her shy midwestern swaying—all erased.

I passed the bowling alley and its little Vegas flourish, and kind of mentally genuflected toward Chimes, although it was only nine in the morning and he wouldn't arrive until God knows when.

Then, more proof that my childhood Minnisapa was just a beta version of what the town would become: a fast food place that sold butter burgers, a car dealership on the edge of the bluff, actually a pickup dealership, dozens of fucking pickups, the whole town had decided they were bubbas. Of course, some son of a bitch in an old sports car was honking beside me. Since I hadn't done anything, I started to flip him off. As I turned, I saw that it was unmistakably Smash, smiling, mouthing something, waving. We pulled over to the shoulder.

It felt great to have someone be this glad to see you.

"Quint, how ya doing?" He hugged me hard enough to dislodge food.

"Fine. Great. My mom had a setback and I'm going down to visit her. How you doing? You look great."

"Yeah, fantastic. I'm working with a guy here, we're kind of partners in an air conditioning business, it's going good."

"Great to hear. You around?"

"Yeah, I'm in the book. Gimme a call. We'll pound some." You gotta love a guy who completely disdains euphemism. We weren't going to have a beer; we were going to pound some. I didn't bother to explain my alcohol situation.

"It'd be great to get together," I said. "I gotta get checked in and stuff and I'll give you a call." I meant it, but I probably wouldn't do it. I get to Minnisapa and the drive and whatever I have to do exhausts me and I just crash at my hotel.

As Smash drove off, he seemed to be saying something. My

guess is that he'd remembered about my mom and was sending his best wishes.

As I pulled out on the highway, I thought: if you're a partner, you don't say you're a "kind of" partner.

When I arrived at the hospital, I was told that my mother had been placed in the geriatric ward.

"I should warn you," the receptionist told me. "Some of the residents there are kind of colorful."

Fuck "colorful." I walked into an asylum for the old. It was dinner time; everybody had been herded together. The smell of shit and urine and disinfectant hit me. Everyone spattered their limp gowns with green or brown or orange goop. They stared at me. Someone yelled, "Son of a shit!" They looked at me as if I had the power to free them. They looked like modern art: A fist of skull here, a nest of cheekbones there; you could see the skeletons asserting themselves. They cawed and screamed and muttered. They didn't have expressions on their faces, just a kind of weather. They were lashed to chairs with ropy mesh vests. Only the maddest ones ignored me. They nodded and drooled and slumped or rocked like fetuses looking for a womb. Their urine pooled in urine-purses. One guy kept repeating "son of a shit"; this and some gauzy silence was all that was left in his brain.

An old woman—her face a part of the body which should be covered; her mouth glistening, smeared—wheeled her wheelchair toward me, so that I had to turn and stop it with my hands. "Be my boyfriend!" she yelled and put her hands on mine. I saw the nurse coming toward me with another demented person in another wheelchair. We were the only two people in the room who knew what year it was.

"I'm Quint King," I said. "Where the fuck is my mother?

Sorry. I'm exhausted. But where's my mom?"

"That's understandable, Quint. She's down the hall. I'm sorry. You caught us at a bad time." She was cheerful.

A plop on my shoulder made me start. A hand like deboned chicken wing. I turned and confronted a geriatric Frankenstein monster: slack mouthed, dim eyed, wedge nosed (as if broken), crew cut.

He said, "Hey, Sarge, you got a cigarette?"

His pants fell down. He wasn't wearing underwear. His dick and the ties from his restraining vest dangled. He didn't seem to notice but looked at me like a dog expecting a treat.

"No, he doesn't have a cigarette, Willie," the nurse said, "And pull your pants up." Actually, we both could have used one.

The nurse pulled Willie's pants up and fastened them with the ties of the restraining vest. "Here, let's go back to your room," she said to him. She said to me, "You can come with us. Willie's room is right next to your mom's."

Then I walked into her room. The woman I saw wasn't my mother. The woman I saw was my mother. Her face geysered fear.

I said, "Mom, it's Quint."

She slurred, "Please."

I said, "Do you know what happened?"

She said something that sounded like, "I didn't do it."

I held her slackened hand and looked into her panicked eyes and told her that I would take care of everything.

People screamed; people negotiated with their insanity. There were a few minutes of silence, then a woman yelled, "Will you shut up!"

A nurse told me that they wanted me to attend something called a care conference, where they explained some therapies and where they also explained that, because she had been alone for so long before they found her, some therapies wouldn't work. After I left the care conference, I drove down a numb frontage road and heard the lacquered friendliness of the hotel clerk of the Holiday Inn at the base of the bluffs. I walked through the pool-smell and down the arrowing hall and threw my bags in the room and didn't open them. I brought my laptop back to the hospital with me. I had no idea when I would have time to write up any notes.

Back in my mom's room, I stepped aside as the nurses emptied her catheter—a pouch filled with liquid the color of melted butter and emptied through gristle-colored tubing. They washed away her shit with wet towels they had spritzed with raspberry-colored, sweet-smelling soap. I could hear her whimper. There wasn't much to do, so I sat there, in the fluorescence and murmur, and looked at the mudslide of her face. I held her damp hand and listened to her breathing. I looked out at the parking lot, which didn't have enough to say.

I could not stand being in the room anymore. I took a drive to the river, bumping through Minnisapa's downtown. I grew up here, but I still get confused about how exactly to get to the river; I passed a gamely struggling coffee house and bagel shop—I'd forgotten how tenacious Minnisapa's hippies were—and a place with what must be 5000 discarded tires and then just walked through an open gate and across some railroad tracks and to a park along the river. I saw the blue hills of Wisconsin in the distance, then the green islands where I had built a boathouse after my dad died; then the water, which was high, so it looked like trees grew upon it. I let the idea of the change of seasons soothe me. In Minnesota, our trees are bare in February; and so full in May that you can feel their growth as slow fireworks, in the moment when the explosion aches toward its apex and then dissipates. But if I were a tree, I wouldn't find their impending death so lovely. I looked instead at the wincing grey water.

When I returned to the geriatrics ward and turned back to my mother it was as if, standing in line for communion, the person that had been in front of me in line had veered away and I confronted the sacrament. I had looked everywhere else: I had looked at her brown-striped hospital gown, at her bulging catheter bag, at her bed rail, at the face of her clock, at the schematic of the parking lot but I turned and saw the small face that had sat on her large body: The knob of chin that had once been what I had seen as I slipped into the house drunk and spied her in her recliner. I saw the now-slackened mouth, the skin both oily and desiccated, the blue ganglia of veins in the white flesh, the surprisingly thin hair, and then I met her eye. Her intelligence struggled like a diver who could no longer remember the surface. My cell phone rang. I let it go, nervously, for now.

CODA

Chimes: One morning the phone has the temerity to ring at some ungodly hour because—I'm pretty sure—one of the punks who works for me is so hungover he knows he won't be able to function this afternoon. So to impress a woman who's been spending a suspicious amount of time in my house, I answer, "This better be good." A voice stumbles then tells me that one Steven A. Sarnia was killed late last night in a one-car accident not that far from where I live, near the old Regal Theater, and that both a cousin and one of the Emergency Room nurses suggested that I be contacted.

"Yes," I say, trying to make up for the way I answered the phone, "Smash and I have been friends since we were kids. My apologies for . . ."

"That's okay, sir," she says. I can tell she's used to the asinine way people answer phones and ignores it just like she ignores the conditions of accident victim's underwear. If you're bleeding nobody cares if you're shitting.

"Would you be willing to identify the body and take care of the arrangements?"

Of course, I say yes. "Is it okay if I get there in about an hour?"

"Of course," the nurse said. She probably thought, "He's dead, you moron" but didn't say it.

I then told the occupant of my bed what happened—she had surmised it from the call—took the worst shower of my life, brushed my teeth as if it mattered, drank the coffee and ate the toast which appeared on my kitchen table and drove to the hospital.

When they pulled the sheet back, I looked at the bruised dregs of my friend and wanted to say, "That's as much him as anyone else" but said "Yes, that's Steven," a name I'd never called him when he was alive.

I spent the rest of the day making calls—first, the practical ones to his cousin, to one of my employees, to Smash's old boss, to an undertaker who bowled Tuesday nights. Then, the even harder calls started. It turned out that I had to call people's parents to get their numbers. At Quint King's mom's house, I left a message on the machine and then just looked him up in Saint Paul. Death meant picking up the phone and getting shit done. It was another day at the office except that sometimes you felt like an abandoned house in December and sometimes you felt the tears swelling up in your eyes and you could see the light twirl in them so you had to take a little I'm-not-going-to-cry break.

The next day, people started showing up at the bowling alley. First, Dickie Burpee who no longer looked like a punch line. Then Quint King who I noticed drank Diet Coke exactly the same way he drank beer back in the day—he'd stare into it, like it held the secret to the universe, then drink half the thing in one swallow. Quint's always been a little brooding, but you could tell that his mom's stroke and Smash's death and God knows what else was on his mind. His cell phone rang, and he said, "Fuck, I've gotta take this." I refilled Burpee's Diet Coke and felt guilty that I'd thought about Smash so much it was actually kind of exhausting and that I was thinking that the woman in my house—her name is Cindy—wasn't going to use this as an excuse to get her hooks in me.

I told this to Quint when he returned.

He looked into his Diet Coke and said, "The nerve of her, making you breakfast."

Just out of my vision, Burpee said, "I think she's nice."

Quint said, "If you didn't like her beforehand, yeah, she's manipulating you and drop her like a hot rock. But don't stop liking a woman because she's nice to you. That way lies madness."

I said, "I can't believe I'm talking about this now. Shouldn't we be having a moment of silence or something?"

"If there's one thing Smash wouldn't want, it would be a moment of silence," Quint said.

Pooch was on a plane now but I know what he would say: "In memory of our friend Smash, we will now enjoy one minute of yelling like idiots."

Quint said, "Me, I feel guilty because tonight I'm going to write a marketing plan for a bagel. Probably sneak away early to do it."

That's when Slow showed up. He normally brings his family everywhere; he flashes the wife and kids the way some guys flash Rolexes. But he came in alone and ordered a beer and, seeing Quint and Burpee, said he'd get their drinks, too. He was a little surprised when I served them Diet Cokes. He'd been trying to be one of the boys. He shook everyone's hand. Quint asked him how his drive was—it's May and the drive is barely 100 miles, so you can imagine how scintillating that was–and then we talked a little about who would show up—everyone but Sarah Hamilton. Quint took a slug off his Diet Coke to hide his reaction to that news and when I refilled it we both shrugged a "women: what are gonna do?" shrug.

We were only able to keep up the small talk for so long. Then, as we sat there like lumps, Quint said, "Weren't we just saying how Smash wouldn't want a moment of silence?"

I said, "I was thinking maybe a moment of yelling like idiots." Pooch wasn't here and it had to be said.

"Or bouncing basketballs off walls so hard they bounce back and knock us out," Slow said.

"When was that?" Quint asked.

"Intramural b-ball. I think junior year."

"Death Before Dishonor," I said. We named the team back when we didn't know anything.

"To the great Death Before Dishonor," Slow said. And we raised three Diet Cokes and a beer and Quint and Burpee became honorary members of that vanished team and the stories started to flow and then, invoking the spirit of Smash, we all started bowling, like we were whipping apple cores through movie screens, like we were still a bunch of monkeys. The pins exploded like fireworks. When Burpee nailed a 7-10 split, Slow high-fived him and said, "Great job, Burps" and Burpee was so pleased to get a nickname, however ludicrous, after all these years that he couldn't stop smiling.

At the memorial service the next day, Slow said some nice things. Mr. Family Man talked about going to a strip club with Smash. I remembered that: somebody's bachelor party, Slow wasn't keen on going but he'd had a couple of beers and we'd dragged him along. I'd remembered it as the time when Smash proposed to the stripper. But I think Slow's version was closer to the truth. Slow said, "My friend Smash—I'm sorry but that's what we called him—said to the dancer, 'You deserve better than this. You can come and live with me' and my friend Smash meant it and I believe that was a fundamentally Christian act and that he acted more honorably than I did in that situation and that is why I will always miss him."

And then I stood up and started talking and I know that what I said must have been okay because some biker chick came up to me three weeks later and said, "You got him right" but all I remember is that I started by saying, "Some of us used to get together for parties" and then I saw Barb Carimona, and she was dressed in a no-nonsense lawyer's suit, but as I met her eye, her face began to shake and moisten and sob, huge sobs that made me stop what I was saying, and she said, "I'm sorry, I'm just really going to miss him," and as out of body as that moment was I finally acknowledged to myself that what we'd always called Barb's ridiculousness was just bravery and I know I'd been planning on closing with my story about the time Smash said, "I've been thrown out of better places than this" but I wound up just mumbling my punch line because something was surging inside of me as I looked at the faces of my friends and I just wasn't sure that maybe this wasn't the best place, after all.

ACKNOWLEDGMENTS

A version of "Crime Prevention" appeared as "Figurines" in the Fall 2000 issue of *Jeopardy*. A version of "Safety" appeared as "Force Majeure" in the Summer 2003 issue of *The Laurel Review*. A version of "Forestry" appeared as "Product Placement" in the *Emprise Review* in the October 2008 online edition.

The merit badge requirements that begin each story are taken from the requirements for the merit badges used in the titles. *2001 Boy Scout Requirements*, Boy Scouts of America, 2001, ©1999

The passage which Quint reads in "Automotive Repair" comes from William James, *The Varieties of Religious Experience*.

The passage which Quint reads in "Cinematography" comes from Woody Allen's *Without Feathers*.

છ૨

Michael Chabon wants Big Star's "Thank You, Friends" played at his funeral. I'm thinking, why wait? I owe thanks to many people, only a few of whom are listed.

To Neal Nixon, Anita Katter, Gary Mahaffey, and Pat Marcotte who provided my first glimpses of tradition, discernment, perseverance, and literary joy.

To everyone who has left helpful marks on parts of this manuscript: Terry Faust, Kai Lahti, Steve Beto, Ric James, Greg Schaffner, Joel Jensen, Daryl Lanz, Jill Crosby, Bill Reichard, Ellen Hawley, David Jauss, David Haynes, Margot Livesey, Bob Lacy, Joanna Johnson, Joe Hart, Carolyn Crook, Matt Helling, Joel Turnipseed, Pepe Demarest, Christi Cardenas, Pamela Johnson, Steve Seefeldt, Amanda Fields, Cheri Johnson, Michael Walsh, Amy Shearn, Marge Barrett, Andria Williams, Rob McGinley Myers, Suzanne Rivecca, and Nan Fulle.

To the Beloit College English Department, especially Tom McBride and John Rosenwald, and the University of Minnesota MFA Program, especially Julie Schumacher and Charles Baxter.

To Pia Z. Erhardt who saw the value in this manuscript, Jim Shepard who selected it, Kim Kolbe and Marianne Swierenga of New Issues who guided it into print, and everyone at AWP especially Supriya Bhatnager.

To the people who've supported me after *Merit Badges*' acceptance, especially: Bill Schuth, Dan O'Shea, Alison Aten, Bryan Bradford, Sari Fordham, Mike Finley, Joe Isaak, Leona Lewis and the Sisters of Anarchy, Emily Powell, Mike Schwartz, Dawn Bentley, Janet Jones, Ann Handley, Sara Schneider, Jerod Santek, Dan Munson, and Janna Radamacher.

To my brother and sisters, who dragged my three-year-old self through the house on a blanket while singing "Hail, Hail to the King."

I owe a special literary debt to Jon Spayde. I owe a profound personal debt to Dave Hultgren and Sue Lenczewski.

And I owe a special debt to you, the reader. The French are right. You are the real author of this book.

photo by Cory Docken

Kevin Fenton lives in Saint Paul, Minnesota and works as an advertising writer and creative director. His fiction has appeared in the *Northwest Review*, the *Laurel Review*, and the *Emprise Review*. His writing on graphic design has been anthologized in *Looking Closer 2* and *Emigre No.70: The Look Back Issue*. He holds an M.F.A. in Creative Writing from the University of Minnesota and a J.D. from the University of Minnesota Law School.

AWP Award Series in the Novel